D0481308

ALSO BY JESSE BALL

The Curfew

The Way Through Doors

Samedi the Deafness

Silence Once Begun

A Cure for Suicide

HOW TO SET A FIRE AND WHY

HOW TO SET A FIRE AND WHY

JESSE BALL

PANTHEON BOOKS, NEW YORK

Library of Congress Cataloging-in-Publication Data
Ball, Jesse, [date]
How to set a fire and why : a novel / Jesse Ball.
pages ; cm
ISBN 978-1-101-87057-0 (hardcover : acid-free paper).
ISBN 978-1-101-87058-7 (eBook).
1. Dysfunctional families—Fiction. 2. Teenage girls—Fiction.
3. Pyromania—Fiction. 4. Arson—Fiction. 5. Psychological fiction. I. Title.
PS3602.A596H69 2016   813'.6—dc23   2015017989

www.pantheonbooks.com

Jacket design by Kelly Blair

Printed in the United States of America
First Edition
2 4 6 8 9 7 5 3 1

For Frank Bergon

Part One

———

IN WHICH I INTRODUCE MYSELF

1

Some people hate cats. I don't, I mean, I don't personally hate cats, but I understand how a person could. I think everyone needs to have a cause, so for some people it is hating cats, and that's fine. Each person needs to have his or her thing that they must do. Furthermore, they shouldn't tell anyone else about it. They should keep it completely secret, as much as possible.

At my last school no one believed me about my dad's lighter. I always keep it with me. It's the only thing I have from him. And every time someone touches it there is less of him on it. His corpse is actually on it—I mean, not his death corpse, but his regular one, the body that falls off us all the time. It's what I have left of him, and I treasure it.

So, I said, many times I said it, don't touch this lighter or I will kill you. I think because I am a girl people thought I didn't mean it.

Someone told me they read in a book that a scientist saw a chimpanzee using sign language on a tree. Apparently the chimpanzee had learned sign language, and then it decided to use the sign language—and it used it on a tree. The amazing thing is, the story ends there. They made the chimp use it with researchers and such—no sign language with trees. I am completely against this sort of thing, and not because I think trees talk or anything—don't worry,

I am very clear-sighted. But still, I bet—you let this chimp talk to the trees and a decade later, well, you don't know what happens, but that's the point.

What I mean is, I have my own plans, my own ideas. Being kicked out of my last school—it didn't really affect them. I guess I don't really care which school I go to. But, I am sorry that I only grazed his neck with the pencil. I thought I could do better than that.

It was a pretty ugly scene. They had me sitting there in the principal's room, with my poor aunt next to me (I live with my aunt—dad = dead, mom in lunatic house) and across from us the principal, and Joe Schott, and his dad and mom. His dad owns a car dealership, which means that everyone respects him, though I don't know why. For instance, the workers at the deli call him *boss* even though he isn't their boss. I've seen it happen.

Anyway, the secretary was there too, taking notes. The secretary is also the gym teacher, and I hate him, so, basically, apart from my aunt, a room full of enemies.

It wasn't lost on me that the principal sat with the Schotts. They started it out in the worst way. The principal said to the secretary, are we ready to begin, and then it was, yes, I think so.

Schott senior said something like, Lucia, we are ready to forgive you, with this horrible expression on his face, and then Joe said, I won't forgive the bitch. I'm going to miss at least two games, and then Schott senior put his hand on Joe's shoulder and started to say something, but the principal cut him off—he said, hold on, let's let her go first. Lucia, are you ready to begin? Do you have something to say?

That's when I said, your little prince basketball hero shouldn't have touched my lighter. Then I wouldn't have put a pencil in his neck.

Well, they didn't like that. Joe Schott is very admired in those parts, the town darling. There's a burger named after him at the diner, and he even has his own house on his parents' property—a "cottage" if you can believe it, which no sixteen-year-old guy should have. I know because a girl I was in study hall with went back there with him (he is good-looking). She is awful also, so I wish them well.

Lucia, if you are going to stay at this school, you must apologize to Joe and to his family.

I am sorry, I said, that I wasn't clearer. Don't touch my fucking zippo, Joe. Eventually, these people are all going to go away and you'll be left alone. Do you understand?

My aunt squeezed my leg, so I didn't say everything I wanted to.

She is really nice. I mean, my aunt is one of the kindest people in the world, I think. She must be. When we got back to the house, she said she was sorry that things had happened that way, with my dad dying, and with my mom going away, but that stabbing somebody wouldn't fix it. She understood the sentiment, she did. Also, she didn't care that I couldn't go back to that school. She would find another school that would take me. The thing she was most glad about was: the police weren't involved. Probably the school had wanted to avoid a scandal. But, a person only gets so many chances.

I love my aunt. She is my dad's older sister and is at least seventy years old, I don't know how. They were dyed-in-the-wool anarchists, she and my dad, that's what my dad used to say. Then, he died and she clammed up. She has enough money to live pitifully and tend a garden. She was so sweet to me, I resolved right then to be no trouble to her ever. We went to a shitty movie theater to watch an old picture about horses. It was a terrible print, and the dialogue was horrid and sentimental. It wasn't *Flicka* or *Black Beauty,* but it was completely ridiculous and awful. Anyway, we both cried a lot at the horse's predicament and then we went back to the house and ate a lot of ice cream with big spoons. She said the big spoons were good on a day like that.

2

You may be wondering why I am giving you this account. Well, I don't know, really. A bunch of things happened, and I am just putting them in order. I'm doing it for myself. You are just a construction—you're helping me to put things in order. You are my fictional audience, and as such I appreciate you very much. I figure when I finish, I will throw this out. Don't think that I believe you are any less terrible than anyone else. That's on you—if you want to behave like a decent person, do so. Those of us who aren't miserable fools will probably recognize it.

Anyway—this is how it went:

My aunt found a new school for me to go to. That school was called Whistler High School. It was the school for the next town over. I could still bicycle there, or take a bus.

I had a month off, and then it was my first day—the start of the next quarter. I didn't like the idea. You might think that I am some sort of hard case. I am just a quiet person who minds her own business. Going to school is terrible and it frightens any right-thinking individual.

That morning my aunt had a surprise for me. I came downstairs and on the kitchen table, there it was—my dad's lighter.

How did you get it?

My aunt winked at me.

I took it from the office the day of the conference. It was there on the desk. I don't want them to have it any more than you do.

What a lady!

Then it was time to go.

I always wear the same thing, so there isn't really much getting ready for me. My aunt has bought me other clothes in the past; I threw them out.

I have:

a gray hooded sweatshirt (hood up)
black jeans
a white tank top
cheap black sneakers
++my dad's lighter++
a notebook & pencil
house key
some money and ID
usually some book
some licorice for if I am hungry

I believe that a person such as myself can live off licorice. Luckily, I have never had to demonstrate the truth of this claim.

When we got to the school, she stopped the car. She said, you look pretty this morning. I said it is because yesterday

I cut my hair like a boy. That's one of those paradoxes you hear so much about. She laughed.

First, I was outside the school. It was big, bigger than the other school. All concrete and glass. I didn't like it. I'm not sure that there's any reason for building anything other than huts. Can't we just live in huts and be kind to each other?

I suppose we'd better go inside.

I could draw my first day at Whistler like a diagram. There is a line that goes across the page a little ways and then it hits a Rorschach blot. When it hits the Rorschach blot it just dies, the line absolutely curls up and dies. Which isn't to say that it went badly.

Here's a sample:

> GIRL So, your name is Lucia. You went to Parkson?
> LUCIA . . .
> GIRL . . .
> LUCIA . . .
> GIRL . . .
> LUCIA . . .
> GIRL I heard you, uh, stabbed somebody with a pencil.
> LUCIA . . .
> GIRL . . .
> LUCIA Yeah.
> GIRL . . .
> LUCIA . . .
> GIRL Uh, I won't tell anyone.
> LUCIA That's okay. You can. It doesn't matter.
> GIRL . . .

There would be a part in the diagram where you could lay a transparency across with little red blots of color to show other things, like—when I noticed kids who seemed okay. I saw a couple of those, but they didn't talk to me. One of them was reading some Trakl, which I thought was okay. I mean, it wasn't a bad sign, at least.

One girl asked me if I was going to go out for sports, which made me spit out the apple juice I was drinking. I said that sports were part of the spectacle. She said what. I said the ruling class. She looked confused. I said otherwise people would get fed up and they couldn't be controlled, so no. I mean, I would go for a run if it was a nice day, or definitely swim. I would do judo or something if they had that. But chase a ball? Do I look like a dog?

I am the captain of the field hockey team, she said.

So, that ended that.

My aunt wanted to know if I had made any friends, and I said that I had made a bunch. She said, tell me about the day. I said:

Well, it started out really well. There was a girl named Kimberly sitting next to me in homeroom and she made me a friendship bracelet. She is in Drama Club and I'm going to be in it, too. We ate lunch together with her boyfriend and a bunch of really nice people. I had so much fun. Then, her boyfriend took us into the back of the gymnasium where no one could see and he inseminated both of us, just like that. It felt really good, not the actual act, but, you know, afterwards, the glow of it . . . So, yeah, I'm pregnant, and I have friends, but no prospects, really.

That's not funny, said my aunt. How did it really go.

Okay, I said. I'll tell you tomorrow.

4

So, I should probably mention a fact. I am really good at guessing how things are going to go. I am a good predictor. I told my aunt that, and she said, like Cassandra? I said, no, because I keep it to myself.

What I am not saying is—I can predict the future. That's garbage. It's this: I have a good way of modeling things in my head, so I can guess how to avoid having to do things I don't want to do, or avoid being involved in things I don't want to be involved in.

For instance, I am always sick when it is time for gym class. Mostly, this works. But I'm not sick right at gym class, no—I get sick during the class prior, so that I have to go to the nurse, and then returning from the nurse (where I turn out to be fine) takes a long time, and then gym class is over, so I am just starting to get changed when it becomes clear I shouldn't bother. This was a point of contention between myself and the gym teacher at my first high school.

Another example: I made friends with the janitors and security guards at the school on my second day. That is, I said hello and offered them some licorice at the entrance to the foul little room where they sit together when they are doing nothing. As simple as that. Now, they like me. They know I'm not like the other shits who attend this school. What does that mean?

It means that when I sneak out the back of the school to go to the store for cigarettes or licorice they won't say anything.

JESSE BALL

12

Also—there is a girl who looks kind of like me whose locker is six lockers down, and I managed to take her license out of her bag when she wasn't looking. Now, if I need to get in somewhere, I can use that, and it will be on the record that she went there.

I think about the future state of affairs, and what will be needed. I know that kind of thinking is foreign to some of you, but you'll have to wise up, chumps! This is the world we live in.

On the second day, a guy asked me on a date. I am definitely not very attractive, that's for sure, but I am pretty skinny and not a leper (my apologies to any lepers out there—not your fault). This guy, he probably figured it was the time to strike, right when I got there. Well, I said we could go out if he wanted, and he said what about for pizza that evening, so we went. He bought me pizza, which was good because I don't have any money. I would rather have bought my own, but what can you do? He got a really big soda, and I asked him if he had a library card. He was mad that the counter guy had *talked to me a little too much.* He said a whole lot of stuff that I didn't hear, and at some point we went outside and I left. He was really tall, so there's that. I looked into the future and I saw that the short guys at the school would figure I only go on dates with tall guys and the tall guys would think she ditched a tall guy after one date, so things were looking good.

Maybe I mentioned that my aunt has a garden? Well, she does. She has a garden wedged in between the house and the garage and a side wall. It looks kind of like this:

```
HOUSEHOUSEHOUSEH  X
OUSEHOUSEHOUSEHO  X
USEHOUSEHOUSEHOU  X
SEHOUSEHOUSEHOUS  X
HOUSEHOUSEHOUSEH  X
OUSEHOUSEHOUSEHO  X
USEHOUSEHOUSEHOU  X
SEHOUSEHOUSEHOUS  X
GARDENGARDENWALL  X
GARDENGARDENWALL  X
GARDENGARDENWALL  X
GARDENGARDENWALL  X
GARDENGARDENWALL  X
GARDENGARDENWALL  X
GARDENGARDENWALL  X
GARDENGARDENWALL  X
GARDENGARDENWALL  X
GARAGENOTHINGNOT  X
GARAGEHINGNOTHIN  X
GARAGEGNOTHINGNO  X
GARAGETHINGNOTHIN  X
GARAGEGNOTHINGNO  X
```

X is the edge of the map. It's important to let people know where the map ends, if you make a map for someone. I read that in a cartography book. Cartography is mapmaking, yeah? It used to be hard and all the maps were mostly wrong, but now it's easy, that's what they say.

So, my aunt's garden. I guess there are two kinds—French gardens and English gardens. Well, maybe there are Chinese and Japanese ones too, but those have mostly moss and stones, so they don't count right now. I'm talking about gardens with plants, yes? So—a French garden, as far as I can tell, is a garden that gets tended. You know, my aunt, she walks around it slowly and bends down now and then to pull up some shit, or to stick some other stuff in somewhere. That's a French garden. An English garden is something that used to be a French garden but that no one does anything to anymore. So, it looks run-down. Things don't grow in proper lines. This is what they tell me. My aunt's garden goes back and forth between these two extremes. Sometimes it is more French, sometimes more English. I asked a French exchange student about this once and he said that English gardens actually aren't gardens. But, he also thinks everyone in France was in the Resistance. To me—an embarrassing number were probably Vichy, and I'm not talking about the ones who got lynched. That's just how it is with history. You do things and later on when people see what you did, it looks bad. The only exception is if you get to defend yourself, but mostly you don't. History is just people behaving badly.

In the diagram you can see that the house is pretty big. That might lead you to think that my aunt is doing pretty well for herself or something like that. When people drop me off, they drop me off in front of this house, and it is a huge house, so they think, well, maybe she dresses like a hobo, but she must be wealthy. I guess it's okay for them to think that. My aunt and I live behind that house and behind the garden. The garage is converted and we live in it, as if it were a little house. It must have been a hassle for my aunt to take me in when they sent my mom up. I sleep in the one bed and my aunt sleeps either in a cot or in this big chair that is in the corner. She often falls asleep reading, so I think it is nice for her.

I mean, I said no way, at first, I will not take the one bed, but since she is actually asleep most times in the chair and there is no one in the bed, I do sleep in it.

One night I woke up in the middle of the night because of the full moon (bright) and thought for at least two hours about my aunt dying and how it would probably happen any day. Of course, the women of this family are long-lived and all that. She will live to be ninety-two in utter misery. That is likely.

I don't think it would be so bad being old, but there are all kinds of things that old people like, they really like them a lot, that I don't like. So, it seems like maybe it isn't for me, at least not yet. I hate thinking about it. Getting older is— you think you are getting your way and you think you are getting your way and you think you are getting your way and then you are old and it turns out you didn't get your way. Or—you did, like my aunt, but the consequences are deeply ironic.

I saw a documentary once about the pyramids and it said that the PB (pyramid builders) were aliens, and that they were essentially cicadas (but bipedal), and that their cycle was ten thousand years rather than ten or fifteen years, and so eventually they would wake up, and, at least the person who was narrating the documentary, he thought that they would be really angry. But, it seems to me that they would be used to things having been ruined while they were sleeping. I don't think they would be angry—not that I believe the documentary. Most documentaries are worse than fiction.

Well, the next day was a disaster. I don't even really want to write about it, but fair is fair, and if I am doing this at all, I might as well put everything down.

I showed up in the morning and they made me leave class to go and see the school psychologist. What's worse, the teacher—who is a fool, I mean, he didn't have to say out loud what it was—said in this awful theatrical baritone voice, *Miss Stanton, Ms. Kapleau would like to see you during first period.* And everyone knows what that means.

So, I had to meet with this Kapleau individual, who asked me about my mom and dad, and pencils, et cetera. And then, when it was over, she asked me if the work was okay or if I maybe should be in a lower grade, which was insulting. I said a dolphin could be valedictorian of this shithole in a heartbeat, and she smiled gently and told me to go back to class.

And that was the beginning of the bad time, because after that, people kept asking me why I had to go to the psychologist, and I had to say because I have a disorder, cataplexy, and that if I laugh, I fall asleep. Which is why I never laugh. Since I never laugh, some of them believed me, except one kid—Stephan—who is smart. He said pretty quietly that it was interesting I should say that, and also, cataplexy is rare, very rare. Luckily, no one listens to him.

The pencil thing hadn't really caught on during my first day, which was good—but now with the psych visit, people were talking about it. I had to eat lunch in a buffer, which is fine. I don't care if I have someone to talk to. But, having people space themselves out in a weird way when you're in line doesn't feel good. I really will stab you if you don't stop, I thought about saying, but—obviously not a good thing to say.

Things took an upturn between fifth and sixth periods when I overheard two kids talking. They didn't know I was there, and the short, dumb-looking one told the bigger one that it had been arranged and the Sonar Club was going to meet at the usual spot that afternoon. They were trying to be real cloak and dagger about it.

I'm sure that doesn't mean anything to you. You're wondering, why is she happy about some Sonar Club. That doesn't sound even remotely fun. Well, I have a friend—I do—who told me about something he heard about from someone else—and what it is, is this:

Right now, there are clubs forming up all over the country. They call themselves sonar clubs, or even radio clubs—but what they are is clubs for people who want to set fires, for people who are fed up with wealth and property, and want to burn everything down.

S - O - N - A - R = A - R - S - O - N

He said you have to burn something down just to get in, and when he said that I thought—I haven't heard something so exciting in a long time. If you don't like fire, you are not a living person, in my opinion.

A really awful thing happened final period, though, in
Social Studies. We were doing a mock trial and I was
supposed to be a witness to a murder, so I was on the
witness stand. One of the supposed lawyers, a girl named
Lisette, was asking me questions. But, she did this mean
thing, a slightly clever mean thing, where she asked me
questions about my actual self. At first, she slipped them
in a little along with the other questions. I wasn't sure
where she was going with it.

*So, you just arrived here at the school. Did you know
the defendant prior to your arrival here? Under what
circumstances?*

2 0

J E S S E   B A L L

There was some chuckling. I said I was not in school
and hadn't been for years—I was supposed to be an old
man. Did she not see my beard? (No one laughed.) I said
I had seen the defendant before, of course. He was one
of my tenants.

*On the night in question, you were out walking the streets
for what reason?*

People laughed again.

I said I wasn't in the street. I was looking out my
window.

That was when she went for it:

I'm sorry, I know it's not a part of the trial, but, how did
you manage to get jeans from four years ago? Did you use a
time machine?

So, Lisette Crowe. It seems that's another person I have to
get revenge on. She is rich but her speech is just television
speech. She doesn't speak like a person with a real mind.
Her parents' money wasn't enough to protect her brain.
I hate listening to the way most people talk. It is enough
to turn you into a hermit. My mother had a beautiful way
of speaking. I like to think about it sometimes.

Anyway, everyone was laughing at me.

Yes, when she said her little nonsense everyone laughed
and I am of two minds about this—is laughing enough to
get you put on the blacklist? I think if you are a shallow
person, essentially a tool for others, then no, you are not
really at fault for laughing. But, I think if you are a person
of greater capacity—not intelligence, you understand,
just wherewithal—then if you laugh, you can indeed find
yourself on the list. Because you didn't have to. Anyway,
I noticed some of those. Consider them added to the list.

By the way—there is nothing wrong with my jeans. I don't
even know what she was talking about. In a blind test, I bet
she couldn't tell them apart from four other pairs.

But, that's the thing—if someone is wealthy and popular,
they don't even have to be right. Whatever they do, they
still win.

8

(which is why they all have to die)

9

At the bus stop after school (it is the city bus), I met a guy who was in college. At least, he said he was. I said I was too, and I think he bought it. He was reading a book about Chernobyl, which seems interesting at first, but actually isn't that interesting. I mean, if you picked up a book like that, you would look at it for a second, and then you would put it down. I don't think you would end up reading it at a bus stop. What's worse is, he was right at the beginning. He hadn't started the book yet. To me, that is a sign that the book is a show-book. Show-books are books that people carry around to seem smart. Anyway, his show-book put me on my guard.

He asked me what I was studying and I said that I was studying the idea of poisons. He asked me what that meant. I said many things are poisonous, but only some of them are poisons. Who gets to decide that cutoff point? Historically, the cutoff point moves around depending on who benefits. I mean—alcohol is pretty poisonous, for instance. He said he liked alcohol. Of course you do, I said.

Do you like to go to shows?

Not really.

Why not?

Because they are expensive. Sometimes my friends and I get in for free.

He said he wasn't surprised that they would let us in for free.

I said that one of my friends is really pretty—so that's probably why.

He said, no, he was saying he wasn't surprised—that he figured I could get in for free, friends or no.

He asked me if I wanted to go to his place, and I said yes, but when it was time to get off the bus, I stayed on it. He got up and he was like, this is the stop. And I just stayed put. I looked out the window. Then, the bus had started up again and he was off it. Maybe I won't ever see him again. That would be okay.

My aunt and I play cribbage sometimes, but she thinks that it is boring, so we have set up a gambling system. Usually you play to 121, and you accrue points in order simply to win. Well, she had the idea (my aunt) that the points could potentially be spent, and that it might make the game more interesting. So, during hands, and between hands, there are ways in which you can use points in order to do a bunch of other things, like nullify cards, or redraw, or double the stakes of a particular game, buy the crib, or double the pegging points. This makes the game very fun. My aunt likes to win. I also like to win. The table that we eat supper on has an inset that you can pull out to reveal a giant cribbage board. We use that when we play. The giant board makes it more fun when you win and less fun when you lose. Whichever one of us is the current victor gets certain privileges in the house. One of those is never doing dishes. Another is getting the blue blanket. At this point, she was the current victor. To be honest, she is usually the current victor. I think she understands the whole thing better than I do. Her claim is that we are both equally good, but this is disproven by the fact that she is the victor more often. I guess it could be true that she is demonstrating some distribution where she is lucky in the early running. Anyway, when she is the victor and she is tired, she sometimes refuses to play because she doesn't want to lose her crown. The conversation that night went something like this:

LUCIA Let's play cribbage.
AUNT MARGARET You promised to tell me about school.

LUCIA Cribbbbbbage. Cribbagggge. [Looks at the floor.]
AUNT MARGARET Oh, here is something for you.

She gave me a notebook with a black felted cover. My old
notebook was just a marble notebook. This one was pretty
obviously superior. I took it and looked at it under the lamp.
I liked it immediately. It is really very nice. Maybe it is the
nicest thing I own—in terms of how much someone else
would value it.

Right then I had a really good idea. I would use the
notebook for writing down my predictions. It would be

THE BOOK OF HOW THINGS WILL GO

I don't know, maybe you think that an idea like that is not
a good idea. I am pretty confident in my predictions, so
it seemed to me like my sum total of happiness would be
improved by having such a book. Not that I need to use the
book to prove to anyone that I was right. I don't tell people
about the predictions, so that isn't a thing.

++

I opened it and wrote on the first page:

THE BOOK

OF HOW THINGS WILL GO

PREDICTION

Leslie is a girl who sits three seats back in homeroom. She has brutal bangs but a wild porcelain doll face and usually wears almost no clothes. She is always talking to a guy, Pierre, who sits next to her. Within the week, she will be horribly maimed in a car accident, and Pierre will never talk to her again. She will then gather her inner resources and become an award-winning physicist. At that point medicine will have advanced and her face will be restored. By then, Pierre will be a homeless drunk and he will pass by a shop and see her being interviewed on a television that is playing in the shop window. Medicine will have restored her face to its exact appearance at the time of the accident, so that despite being thirty-eight at that point, her face is sixteen and hot, really hot, and this will yank Pierre's heart actually out of his chest so that it flops around on the ground like a trout. People walking on that street will cautiously step around his prone body. Meanwhile, she still secretly loves him, and when she happens upon his body at the local morgue while enjoying the good times with some hard-drinking friends, she can't deal with the pain. She runs out into the street and is mauled by a car for the second time! Meanwhile, Pierre wasn't dead—but just asleep. He stumbles out of the morgue and finds Leslie's mauled body where nine or ten cars have run it over. He fails to recognize her, but what he does see is: miraculously, the pint of scotch she was drinking is unharmed, tucked as it was into the side of her skirt. He kneels to remove the whiskey, and is overwhelmed with fabulous good feeling.

Just kidding! That isn't how the predictions go.

The predictions are more like:

Tomorrow I will go to the Home to visit my mom. I will
wear a raincoat and I will take the number 12 bus all the
way down Ranstall Avenue and change to the number
8 at Bergen. While I am riding the bus, I will read a
collection of short stories about insects. One of them is
"The Metamorphosis," so you can see that the book is more
entertaining than it sounds because the editors have given
themselves a wider purview. While I am reading that book,
which is an Ace Book and says it was once sold for 45¢,
someone will try to talk to me. I will grunt and indicate
that I am reading a book. When I get to Stillwell, I will
get off the bus. No one else will get off it because no one
else will be on it at that point. I will walk half a mile to
the entrance, and then half a mile past the gates to the
main building. At the main building, I will get a guest pass
and I will be escorted to my mother's room. She will not be
in the room. I will then be escorted to the fish pond. She
will be sitting in a rocking chair next to the fish
pond. She will be wearing a medical gown. Her hair will
be in a ponytail (she never wore it in a ponytail). I will
approach her and speak to her. She will once again fail to
recognize me. I will sit with her for a while until it becomes
clear that it isn't doing anyone any good. Then, I will go
back and hand my pass in. I will walk back down the
drive. I will walk to the bus stop. I will get on the number 8
bus. I will take the number 8 bus past Ranstall, past
Wickham, past Arbor, to Twelfth. There I will get out. I will

go into the bowling alley, Four Quarter Lanes, and I will sit at the bar and my friend Helen will pour me a drink. She used to be my babysitter when I was a kid. She is forty-five and is writing a book about self-hypnosis. I always go to see her after visiting my mom.

WHAT HAPPENED

I woke up late and when I got to school third period I didn't
have an excuse, so I got a detention. Really, I guess—if we
are being completely honest, I got a detention for asking
Mr. Beekman why he was unhappy that I wasn't on time.
He said that I was supposed to be in school. I said, but why
are you unhappy about me not being in school. He said
because I need to get an education. I said that the whole
thing was a farce. Did he believe that the American public
was educated? Was that his argument? That he is helping to
educate the population of a democracy—and that he wants
me to be there at the start of first period so I can do a good
job voting some years from now when he is being wheeled
around in his old-age home? At this point, he gave me a
detention and made me sit down.

That whole business made Stephan want to pass me a note,
I guess, since he did. The note said, not-a-democracy-ha.
The girl, Stephanie, who passed it to me—yes, that's right,
Stephanie passed me the note from Stephan; I don't know;
people should come up with better names for their fucking
children, it's not my job—anyway, Stephanie tried to look
at the note, but the writing was really small so she couldn't
read it.

The point is—and how this lines up with the prediction
(1) is that I had detention after school—right at three. So,
there was the question, will I go to detention? I wasn't
sure what would happen if I didn't go. Maybe I would get
another detention? If so—that just means I get to schedule

when my detention is by going or not. Probably, they give me two. Each one not gone to means two. I bet that's it.

Well, I didn't go. Sure enough, three p.m. I got on the bus, number 12—then bus number 8. I had my raincoat—I always wear it when I visit her because I saw a film, *Rascal Sven,* about an old Swedish man who goes to a mental asylum, or is put there, and someone comes to visit him (his brother) wearing a raincoat. Then that guy—Sven's brother, who is really kind, evidently they all love each other in Sweden—gives Sven the raincoat, and so Sven leaves in the raincoat and his brother stays at the mental asylum, and when Sven has gotten away, the brother says that he is not Sven and they have to let him go. There is a lot of singing in the movie but it isn't a musical. Sven just sings these shitty little songs when he does something clever.

So, I figured—maybe I have the raincoat, maybe I'm there, maybe my mom recognizes me, and I can give her the raincoat—then she can get away, go somewhere. I don't even need to see her. I just don't like the idea of her sitting by the fish pond.

So, I read my insect book, and this time it was a story about a scientist who alters his DNA to grow a huge fly eye on his forehead. He ends up going insane because he can't sleep since the eye can't ever close. In my opinion, a terrible story. I walked up the drive, got my pass from a girl who looked nearly the same age as me. My mom's room was not what I expected. It had been moved, but she wasn't there.

So, we went down to the fish pond, and there she was, hair in a ponytail. The orderly who escorted me there, a kind of wiry guy in his twenties, asked me about my book so I gave it to him. That's the kind of thing I like to do sometimes.

I sat with my mom and she did some gurgling. I thought about how it was easy to think it meant something— the gurgling, but it was actually like leaves or gravel or layers of skin. I mean to say—it isn't meaningful, it isn't meaningless. Things just don't really apply to us in particular, even though we want them to.

The orderly came back and he had an applesauce. I think his idea was that I could give it to my mom. It was nice of him—and probably just about the limit of his resources there as an orderly, this applesauce gift, but I wanted nothing to do with it. He could see that, so he didn't offer it to me. I don't know, maybe he was just going to eat the applesauce and he forgot I was there at the fish pond. Certainly, my mom wasn't going to tell on him. Practically anything could happen right in front of her and she wouldn't notice.

So, I walked back down the drive, took the bus to the bus to the bowling alley. I was wrong before, by the way, about someone talking to me. No one talked to me on the trip there, and no one talked to me on the trip back. At 4QL Helen made me a Manhattan and I was instantly drunk. I sat slumped in one of the pleasantly curved plastic chairs for about two hours watching people bowl until she was finished and then she drove me home.

PREDICTION

So, I made a prediction while I was drunk at the bowling alley. It wasn't much of a prediction. It was this: I would get home and my aunt would say that the school had called because I didn't go to detention and then I would say that I had gone to the Home and then she would notice that I was drunk and she would thank Helen for bringing me. What she wouldn't do is: yell at me for skipping detention, yell at me for being drunk, yell at Helen for giving me alcohol.

My aunt has some rules for the house. They are pretty similar to the rules my dad had when we all lived together. The first rule is, *Don't do things you aren't proud of.* Just don't do those things. If you end up getting in trouble because of it, then the whole group of us deals with that problem together. But, there is no reason to do things you aren't proud of. All right, that's rule one. Rule two is: *Don't believe nonsense, and don't behave like a robot.* It's much better to get in trouble than it is to be a robot, because the effects of being a robot are difficult to remove.

These rules aren't ever stated—there isn't a rule sheet. It's just the way things are. As long as I am keeping to them, my aunt will stick up for me, I'm sure of it. She isn't disappointed in me. I really think she thinks I'm doing a good job. I think so too, but probably the two of us are alone in that. Even Helen gives me a sad look when she sees me. Probably she thinks I will become a prostitute. Well, she knows I'm not one yet—because I never have any money to pay her for the drinks she gives me!

Another rule is: *Don't pay attention to property, but be mindful of people's investment in things.* This one is a little tricky. It's like—I mean, obviously you can't own anything. So, there is no stealing. My aunt doesn't care if I steal from the supermarket or whatnot. She might be mad if I got caught in a stupid way, but that's just because she has an expectation of my cleverness. Sometimes I can be clever. Anyway—there is no stealing because you can't own anything, so stealing isn't stealing, it's just taking something that you can use. However—if someone puts their life into something, then maybe you shouldn't take it. They call it *sabi* in Japanese—it is when a thing shows the use of a hand. If there is a guy who has a guitar and it sits in his house and he never uses it, my aunt would be fine with me showing up at home with the guitar, if I am going to play it. But if not, then I am kind of an asshole for taking the guitar, or at best, neutral and a bit covetous. Now, on the other hand, if a guy has a guitar and he plays it all the time and you can see that his hands have changed the guitar—that it is *his* guitar, really, then it isn't right for me to take it. If I really needed a guitar, maybe he would give it to me. That kind of thing happens, but that would be up to him.

There is a rule also about being considerate, which is basically just making sure to have empathy. So, that extends to things like cleaning up after myself, which I am not always good at. This is where I get in trouble. But, getting in trouble isn't so bad. It just means my aunt glares at me a little.

WHAT HAPPENED

We got back and the school hadn't called, so my aunt didn't tell me that they had. She did notice that I was drunk, because she put on the pot for tea, which is what she does when I am drunk. Otherwise she asks me if I want tea before putting on the pot.

Also, she did ask Helen if she wanted to stay for tea and thanked her for bringing me home. Helen declined and headed out. I think her book about hypnosis is going to be terrible. She has maybe twenty books about hypnosis at her house. I know because I have been there. Her "book" is mostly just parts she likes from the other books that she has copied into a new book. There is nothing wrong with that, but it isn't really an achievement. I guess if it is a fundamental improvement, it would be. If all the other books were redundant because of her book, then it is a pretty succinct business, so I guess that would be something. But, it's about hypnosis, which I don't believe in anyway.

They had a hypnotist come to our school, to the last one, Parkson, and some people got onstage and he made them pretend to be farm animals and contort into weird positions. The math teacher stood on his head, which is something apparently he can't do. I don't know what that proves. The whole thing left me feeling a bit sick.

PREDICTION

I thought about the guy from the Home while I was
lying there drunk in the chair holding the tea my aunt
made me. I couldn't drink it because it was too hot, but
I was holding it and it was kind of like a hot water bottle.
We have one of those, my aunt and me, and we use it in
the winter. Actually, I think my aunt uses it year-round,
which doesn't make sense. The window next to the
chair is cracked at the top and mended with tape and
there is a bit of a draft, which makes the glass brush
back and forth. I like to listen to it when I sit in the
chair.

It was great of him to bring me the applesauce. It's
probably the first nice thing someone has done for me in
a while. He was wearing that awful uniform that the
Home makes its employees wear, but it looked okay. I
mean, it looked good. I'm sure he is completely deluded.
Most people can't keep all the lies straight—and they end
up believing everything. I promise myself every day that
won't happen to me. He is probably in his late twenties.
I don't know.

I wrote down a prediction then, before I went to sleep,
and it was:

Tomorrow I will find out more about the Arson Club.

This is a pretty shitty prediction, if you ask me. I think
I shouldn't do predictions when I have been drinking.

Of course, it is possible that such a thing could happen. I could find out more about the Arson Club. But there is no reason to think it would happen. I hate when I break my own rules. What's the point of me being rational if I flail around like a clown?

WHAT HAPPENED

Stephan, it turns out, is probably also in the Arson Club.
I know this because of what happened in Social Studies
class. We had to turn in a *topic for research* and then we had
to go to the library and use the computers or look up books
about the subject. Most of the kids are useless cretins, so
they wait in a line while the librarian does all the work for
them. First thing I do when I get in a library is—I go to the
stacks and nose around. The idea is—you don't know what
you're interested in. That's why it's possible to be surprised.
So, instead of looking for things in particular, you look for
what you didn't know you liked, and then when you find
it you know that you liked it, and then you are a broader
person than you were before.

That's what I was doing nosing around in the book stacks.
Stephan was maybe doing the same thing. I had a slip of
paper and it said, Russia Peasant Fire-Setting. There were
some numbers, too, for the place the materials might be.
I had walked back and forth, nosing around, until I got
tired of doing it, and decided to find what I was actually
looking for—and when I did, there was Stephan, looking
at the same shelf. He was holding a book called *Arson
Investigation, Step by Step.* He almost dropped it when
I came around the corner.

STEPHAN What are you looking for.

LUCIA . . .

STEPHAN . . .

LUCIA I don't know. Why?

STEPHAN . . .

LUCIA . . .

STEPHAN I don't know.

LUCIA Excuse me, the book I want is right here.

I took it off the shelf and handed it to him.

?

You asked what I was looking for.

Stephan looked at the book and looked at me thoughtfully. I had my hood up, so I felt pretty good. I wondered if I should ask him about the Arson Club, but I didn't. Next thing I know, we are all just back in class, and then I get called to the principal for having skipped detention, and then I am told: you have a week of detention. They don't understand—I can just read a book. It doesn't really matter where I am. The principal's assistant actually takes me to the detention, as if he is afraid that I will run off into the woods.

In my head, I imagine the conversations that they have probably had at their country club with the old principal from Parkson. *Little hellion stabbed him with a pencil, watch out. Yeah, he's the best basketball player we've ever had.* That and other nonsense I'm sure they say.

Anyway—it turns out that detention was the place to go if you want to join the Arson Club. Which makes my drunk prediction right. I'm not really comfortable with that.

THE ARSON CLUB

Do you want to know how detention works? You go to a classroom and there, voilà, all the other shitty little fucks produce themselves like rabbits out of a hat. Then you are supposed to sit together doing nothing as punishment for not obeying. Maybe you can see from this that I am quite familiar with being in detention. Matter of fact, I feel like I have always been in detention. I am an old veteran of detention, like one of Napoleon's soldiers limping back from the battle of Moscow. No, not like them—they were chumps. More like—one of the girls who died in the Triangle Fire looking out the window and realizing it is too far to jump, then jumping.

So, you sit there and you are supposed to be stupid, so they don't expect you to better yourself. You're not allowed to talk, because they don't think what you say to each other could be useful, even to their mission, as they pretend it to be (that we are bettering ourselves). I suppose they just think we will make trouble if we talk, which is true. But, the trouble we will make is unavoidable.

Let's talk about DAY ONE, DAY TWO, DAY THREE, DAY FOUR, and DAY FIVE because those are all the detentions I serve that week, and nothing else that happens at school is interesting. In my classes I have my hood up and I sit and write in my notebook. At lunch I sit by myself. I have zero interactions and people have decided to leave me alone, which is partly due to a photograph someone got from someone else—I guess they know people at Parkson. The

photograph was pretty funny. I don't have a phone, so
I couldn't get the picture for myself, but I would have liked
to have it.

It seems like somebody took a picture of me when I didn't
notice. Then they stuck cat eyes on my face and claws on
my hands and put in a thought bubble, and in the thought
bubble they put a picture of Joe Schott's actual neck with
the cuts from the pencil. So, I guess that other picture had
been making the rounds at Parkson, and some genius here
decided to be even funnier. Well, I liked it—that much I'll
say. I wish I could have showed it to my aunt or my dad.

DAY ONE

I sat and read *The Theatre and Its Double* by Artaud.
At first I thought it was just about theater, but then
I realized Artaud probably hated theater. Or he hated
other people's theater. He wanted to rescue theater
from the philistines, which is everyone. So, I sat and
read that. I ate licorice. I saw that one of the guys I had
seen talking that time, he was sitting next to me. We
can sit wherever we want, but we can't talk and we can't
move once we sit down. Janine Pezaro, for instance, sits
at the front. She doesn't care if people sit behind her
because she is a brick shithouse and can beat up half
the guys in the school. Probably more than half. She is
in here for beating up two girls at the same time. I am
sort of in love with her for that. But, she is definitely
deluded.

The guy had mentioned the Sonar Club, and now he
was sitting near me. I left the book *All Russia Is Burning*
out on the desk next to the Artaud, and asked if I could
go to the bathroom. They gave me a five-minute pass
(that's really only enough time to get to the bathroom
and back). When I returned to my seat, I saw that he
had taken the book from the desk and was reading it.

Give me that back.

He handed it over. *Sorry, it looked interesting.*

Ms. Kennison yelled at us for talking, so we shut up.
A seed sown. There was still the question of if they let girls

in the Arson Club. I could imagine some bullshit misogynist nonsense governing this also. My aunt was always telling me—never accept any privileges that are for girls, because it is only half the coin.

DAY TWO

Fatty wasn't there, so I just read. This time it was some Alfred Jarry that I found in a church bin. Apparently he would carry a revolver around and threaten to use it on people.

DAY THREE

Not a good day. I spat on Lisette at lunch, and got detention for that, because, as it turns out, her mom is the guidance counselor and she has some kind of pull. So, when I show up for detention as usual, Kennison does a little chuckle, and says, I guess you'll be a regular here for a while, like we have some joke in common. I'm not one to divide myself off from the rest of humanity, I mean, I would like to help them, but let's be clear—Kennison and I are not in the same boat, no way. So, I just go and sit. I ran out of licorice the day before, and Green Gully ran out too, so I didn't have any. To explain: there are two stores that sell the licorice I like. One of them, I can steal from. The other I have to have money. Now, my aunt has almost no money, so I can't use the almost no money she has to buy licorice. That means, I only get licorice when Green Gully has it. They are a fancy supermarket, which means they charge so much they don't need to have proper security.

By the way, I don't think spitting on people is that great, but Lisette said something about me living with my grandma, which I didn't like. All the time—all the time, people basically beg me to freak out on them, and mostly I keep my cool.

DAY FOUR

This is the day when I realize that the girls who sit at the other corner in the back alternate smoking a joint in the bathroom essentially the entire time they are in detention. They do this by repeatedly asking to go to the bathroom and claiming they have their period. I thought that was funny, when I saw them doing it, but I didn't understand. Then, when I was actually in the bathroom to use the bathroom, I saw one of them, and she offered some to me. So, that made the detention go by pretty quick. In fact, I was high for maybe two hours, so after detention, I went with them to a park, and we watched a homeless guy chase seagulls. At some point, we had been watching him do it for maybe twenty minutes, Lana says, I think he's chasing the seagulls, which made us all laugh until we cried. Even I laughed at that, and I never laugh.

DAY FIVE

I decided on this day to just do the research paper, even though it would be three weeks ahead of time. So, I browsed through the Russia book and wrote up a gloss of what the paper would be. Then, I wrote the first few pages. The position of the author as far as I could tell is that peasants burned down their own houses not for political reasons, but out of ignorance, and sometimes as vengeance for minor slights. This was a bit depressing, but seemed almost inevitable. There was a part about peasant women waking up early in the morning to take their babies out of the iron stove where they had put them in the night. Yes, they put their babies inside an iron stove full of coals. So, if you see a Russian person doing something crazy, as you sometimes do, remember—they have been doing that shit forever. It's nothing new.

On day five, which was Friday, I should say—I found a note in my locker. It said—11 p.m., Alcatraz.

Alcatraz isn't really Alcatraz, of course. It's just a little island that is in the middle of a lake in one of the medical parks. Kids like to go there to drink.

ALCATRAZ

My aunt doesn't mind if I go out late, because I mostly don't
go anywhere. She thinks that if I'm out late, then maybe I
have some friends. In her mind that outweighs the dangers
of being out late, whatever those might be. As it turns
out, when I am out late, it is just that I am sitting in a park
somewhere, or in a cemetery, or even at a laundromat.
You know, places where people go when they don't know
anyone.

That meant I could very easily go to this meeting if I felt
like it. I stopped at home to drop off the library books and
I got a screwdriver from under the sink. My aunt wasn't
even there—on Friday she volunteers at a shelter; I think
it's some kind of soup kitchen. The other people who work
there are religious and she can't stand them, but she goes
anyway. She's like me—she doesn't know very many
people, and so she gets stuck with the ones she does know.

I had to take the bus to the medical park, because it was
pretty far from the house. I had been there twice before,
both times with older guys, when I was still in middle
school. It looked different when I was by myself, but I found
the way.

The first part is—getting past the security booth that is by
the main road. To do that, you walk about two hundred
feet down along the fence, and there is a spot where there
just isn't any fence. The fence has broken and you can walk
through. Why they don't fix it—I don't know. So, you go

through there, and there is a path that leads to the internal road. While going along the internal road, you have to keep an eye out for the guard, but since he goes around in a truck with lights, there is always enough time to jump in the bushes. Eventually, you get to some woods, and you go through the woods. There isn't really a path. For some reason no plants grow there, so you can walk where you want. Eventually you get to the island. If you go the wrong way, there is a swampy part and your shoes will get wrecked.

The island can be reached by climbing along a branch that goes about four feet above the water for something like twenty feet. At the end it goes into the water, but there are stones you can jump on. It sounds difficult, but it is pretty easy, especially if you are at all agile. To be honest, the island shares almost nothing with Alcatraz. Kids have been calling it that for a decade at least, though.

From the shore, I could see that there were some people out there. I went along the branch, jumped to the rocks, jumped to the bank. There I was. A kid came up—it was Stephan. He had on an insulated flannel shirt so I didn't recognize him. He must have been waiting for me.

We're over here.

He pointed to the right a ways. Once I was there, I could see there were a few groups of kids sitting on rocks. We went up to the crest of the hill and there was a pretty big tree next to a broken-down shack. The shack had writing on it. I couldn't see it this time, but I knew from before. The writing (I don't know if it is still there) said, Joan fecks goats. When I saw that, my first thought was that a Scottish person had written it, but I looked closer, and the *e* is just a screwed-up *u*. I'm not even sure Scottish people say *fecks*.

By the tree and the shack, in the darkness, there were a bunch of people, maybe ten. Stephan introduced me to them, but he did it the way you do when you don't even know the people—essentially when you yourself need to be introduced, but there's no one to do it for you, so you introduce someone else. It is a shitty way to behave.

This is Lucia.

One of them asked me in a sarcastic voice if I liked fire. I thought it was pretty hokey to do it, but I was holding my dad's zippo in my hand and I flipped it open real quick and lit it. I did it real quick, I must say. It was some legerdemain.

A few of the kids clapped. One said, yeah, that's it. You'll do fine. Someone else asked Stephan if I was his girlfriend, and we both said no.

One of the guys wanted to see the zippo, so I let him. He fumbled with it a bit and gave it back.

I sat down by the tree, and Stephan sat too. The lights of the drive that wound through the medical park marched through the trees in a winding pattern. Beyond that were more lights—the city, the highway, more lights and more.

This terrible little island we were on was a nice mote of darkness. I could hear the water.

I couldn't see the other people too well—it was pretty dark, but they looked mostly older, maybe seniors. One of the guys on the other side of Stephan asked him when he was going to qualify. Qualify? I figured that meant setting the fire that would make him an official member. Stephan didn't say anything. I wondered how many members there were.

Noise from the other side of the island filtered through the trees. Some people were shouting—another group had just arrived. Someone set off some fireworks—or it was a gun, I don't know.

The same guy was talking again to Stephan. I leaned in to hear. He said, you have a month to set a fire, and if you don't you're out.

He saw me looking at him. *Same goes for you.*

I met his eyes and nodded like it was nothing.

He told Stephan to move so he could sit next to me, and Stephan did.

PREDICTION

Well, I saw Stephan that Monday in front of the school. He was standing by himself kicking a stone against a wall. The ground there was all mashed flat and dusty and nothing was growing. He kicked the stone back and forth. It was kind of mesmerizing. I asked him if the meetings were always in the same place.

He said he'd never been to Alcatraz before. He had been to two other meetings—at a guy's house. Real members have meetings with prospective members, and then the real members have their own meetings. I asked him how he had found out about it. He said it was through his brother, who was overseas in the army.

He said: I went to Stuart Rebos's place about a month ago. Two other guys were there. We talked about setting fires. Neither one of them had done a big fire yet. Then, Jan showed up—the guy you met. He told us about some techniques and gave us a pamphlet that someone else had given him.

I asked him how old Jan was. He said he thought he was about twenty-four. Definitely he had gone away to college. Stephan said Jan had been his brother's friend, but that they had for the most part lost touch.

First period that day was a study hall for me, so I sat and wrote in my prediction book.

Jan will try to sleep with me if I am alone with him. Don't be alone with him.

I wrote also,

Stephan isn't as smart as I thought he was,

which isn't a prediction.

OWNING THINGS

About owning things. If you try to own things, but you
don't have very many things, then you can get in trouble.
Because you might have to trade in some of the things
that you *have* in order to get the money to get part of
something new, but then when you run out of things that
you *have* to trade to get money to give to finish getting the
thing that is something new, then you have no money to
finish getting that thing—the new thing, and then someone
comes and takes the new thing, and then somehow, you
have nothing, even though you did start with a bunch of
things (however shitty they may have been—they still
were yours).

Maybe it will make more sense if I give an example. My
aunt got a car, but she only has money for food (someone
she knows lets us live in this garage, so she doesn't pay
rent). She doesn't really have money to pay for the car. I
think she got it in order to *take me around to where I need
to go* and such things. I remember her saying something
like that. Maybe she thought that because she is old we
couldn't go around together without a car. Anyway —she
had to sell her jewelry from when she had a husband a
hundred years ago (he died when she was still nineteen,
a year after they got married). She had to sell her clarinet
and her piano. It was not a nice piano—just a tuneless
little upright, but she played it all the time.

Once she had sold those things, there wasn't anything
else to sell. She missed some payments, then people were

calling on the phone about it for a while. That brings us to
Saturday morning.

We woke up and there were two really big guys outside.
They broke into her car and drove it away. I yelled a bunch
of stuff at them and tried to call the police, but my aunt
said it was useless. *The repossession men and the police have
an understanding.* One of my favorite books was in the
back of the car, too, and that they stole. Maybe the car was
theirs to take, I don't know. But the book, *Barbarian in the
Garden,* by Zbigniew Herbert, that was my book, and there
is no way they were ready to appreciate it. You have to read
probably five hundred books before you can read that one.

My aunt said now I had a good thing to look forward to.
What was that? She said now when I go to used bookstores
eventually I will find it and there will be a kind of reunion.
In the meantime, there are plenty of other books to read.

She didn't even complain about the car—not once. I was
hoping she would shoot them. That's what was in my mind
when I saw how big they were. I know she has a pistol. It's
because of what happened to my father and mother. She
isn't a violent person, but being the first one there (I was
at a friend's house when it happened), I think it was hard
for her. By the time I got home, past the police, and so on,
there wasn't anything to see, so I never saw it. My mom was
already in the hospital; my dad was at the morgue. I am
glad I didn't, because it really fucked my aunt up. But, I am
also a bit jealous, because I feel like it was my thing to see
and I never saw it.

PREDICTION

My aunt will say in about ten minutes that we should walk
down to Muscha Park and feed the pigeons and read and
then afterwards eat a hot dog from a vendor. We will then
go to the park and we will sit and feed the pigeons some
bread that we got for free from a bakery and we will read
and afterwards we will eat a hot dog from a vendor. That
is—one hot dog for the two of us.

I wanted to be vegetarian once, but it isn't in the cards.
Buying nice vegetables is pretty expensive. Maybe one day.

When I think about what my future holds, it is a bit like
looking into the sun. I flinch away, or I don't and my eyes
get burned down a bit, like candles, and then I can't see
for a while.

The way we have things laid out—it makes it easy to know
how to behave, but it isn't so clear that I will be a success.
I have no intention of going to college. Someone told me
about a program that is at a school near us, a good school.
The program sounded neat, so I read one of the professor's
books. He is a real big shot, and gets prizes, goes to fancy
places. There is a picture on the school's site of him shaking
hands with the president, if you can believe it.

His book was terrible. It was intellectually weak. I don't
think his brain is very strong—or somewhere along the
way it got polluted. Not to mention that he fraternizes with
petty oligarchs.

My question is—why would I go to study with someone like that. I have no intention of bowing intellectually to such a person. My aunt says that I am vain and that I boast, but she doesn't know that I talk to no one.

WHAT HAPPENED

It went just like that. My aunt was feeling pretty bad about
the car. I don't think she cares about having a car, but I
think she was embarrassed for me, because it will be hard
for me at school to live in a garage and be broke and have
no car. It won't be hard for me in a metaphysical sense—
I can handle it. But, people will turn against me. Public
opinion, if you will.

She is cheerful, though, so after a few minutes, she asked
if I wanted to get some air, and I said yes, and we went out
and down the street. Most people would be pretty stressed
out about having to go somewhere with my aunt, because
she looks pretty weird. She wears a hat that—let's just say,
I have no idea where she got this hat. She has a turquoise
coat and she wears those huge black sunglasses that
can cover other glasses, but since she doesn't have other
glasses, I'm not sure why she does it.

I should say, I was sad once when I went with her to a
restaurant and we saw a girl from Parkson. It was a girl
who I thought was smart and maybe could be my friend,
but once she saw my aunt, I knew it wouldn't happen. I felt
bad about it—this was the combination:

part of me felt angry at my aunt for causing it;

part of me felt awful that I wouldn't get this friend;

part of me felt okay because obviously the girl was terrible
if she cared so much about what other people think that
she would disqualify me on the basis of my aunt.

The whole thing was even worse because it was supposed to be a celebration. I had this problem for a while where I couldn't stop crying, so I was out of school for two months and just crying all the time. It made me get brutal headaches. This was the first two months that I lived with my aunt, after the thing happened. So, at the end of that time, when a week or two passed, and I wasn't crying anymore, my aunt said we should celebrate. Even though we couldn't afford to, she knew it was the right thing to do—so we went to a restaurant. That's when this happened, which made me feel even worse. Because my aunt is great. Fuck anybody who doesn't approve of her!

Of course—I expect that I will look as strange to people as my aunt does if I live as long as she has. I think back then it looked to me that there was a chance I would be able to go undetected—that I could pass through society without being noticed. Since I realize now that people are against me anyway, it is easier for me to stomach having people think my aunt is a freak.

So, ultimately, I can't take credit for being okay now with my aunt's weirdness, is what I'm saying. I've just accepted that we're painted with the same brush.

We walked down to the park. There were no pigeons. I don't know where they had gone to, but when we tossed some bread on the ground, there were many pigeons. My theory is—they hide inside the park benches and wait.

If you want to say, Lucia, there is no inside of the park benches, I won't argue with you. But, then you have to say where the pigeons come from.

After that, we read—I read a book about cremation in China. My aunt read *Faust* in German. The hot-dog guy gave us two hot dogs because he felt bad for us when my aunt had to pay for the one hot dog with change.

I want to add about my aunt that she does everything with an immense amount of dignity—so it isn't that she really looks like a weirdo. It is just that people have so little acumen these days—they don't even know what dignity looks like. Or, a few do. Like the hot-dog guy. He was moved by her display.

PREDICTION

Tomorrow I will go to the Home to visit my mom again.
I will wear a raincoat and I will take the number 12 bus all
the way down Ranstall Avenue and change to the number
8 at Bergen. While I am riding the bus, I will read more
in my book about Chinese cremation. While I am reading
that book, someone will try to talk to me. I will grunt and
indicate that I am reading a book. When I get to Stillwell,
I will get off the bus. No one else will get off it because no
one else will be on it at that point. I will walk half a mile
to the entrance, and then half a mile past the gates to the
main building. At the main building, I will get a guest pass
and I will be escorted to my mother's room. She will not
be in the room. I will then be escorted to the fish pond.
She will be sitting in a rocking chair next to the fish
pond. She will be wearing a medical gown. Her hair will
be in a ponytail (she never wore it in a ponytail). I will
approach her and speak to her. She will once again fail to
recognize me. I will sit with her for a while until it becomes
clear that it isn't doing anyone any good. Then, I will go
back and hand my pass in. I will walk back down the drive.
I will walk to the bus stop. I will get on the number 8 bus. I
will take the number 8 bus past Ranstall past Wickham,
past Arbor, to Twelfth. There I will get out. I will go into the
bowling alley, Four Quarter Lanes, and I will sit at the bar
and my friend Helen will pour me a drink. This time I will
try to drink it a little slower. Probably, I will drink a glass
of water first. (If I am hungry or thirsty and someone gives
me a beer or a mixed drink, I will almost always drink it
too fast, or faster than I should.)

WHAT HAPPENED

I woke up and made my aunt breakfast. That was—a
poached egg. My mom showed me once how to do it. It
requires a bit of a skillful maneuver. There was a little left
of a fancy pepper, so I used it for her egg and ground it over
the plate. The pepper ground up really beautifully. When
I get to use nice things, I always think: nice things are so
nice. But, like everything else—you get used to them and
they vanish, unless like me you never get them, or only
rarely.

She was really happy about the egg. When I got to her
with it, she was already sitting up, since she slept in the
chair, so it was just a matter of her opening her eyes and
being happy.

I had my raincoat on, and she knew where I was going.

Later, chief! she said. It was a joke from an old TV show
that aired fifty years ago. I always laugh and enjoy
pretending to enjoy the joke, even though I don't know
what it is.

Later, I said.

I took the number 12 to the 8. I read my book. Three
people tried to talk to me separately. I got rid of them
by doing nothing. I walked up the drive to the main
building. The girl was there, and she gave me a weird
look along with the pass. The orderly came, same guy

as before, and he was happy to see me. I could tell even though he acted like it was nothing at all. He said he had read the book. Did he like it? He said some of the stories were good but some were very bad. I said this is true—this is the way it is with that book. We went down to the fish pond straightaway, which was new. When he left he patted me on the shoulder, where the raincoat had fallen off. Which meant, he touched my shoulder, and I could feel his hand there while I sat looking at my mom. She was looking at the pond.

She does this thing where she is looking at the pond, and then for no reason she wants to go closer, so she gets out of her chair and leans over the pond, looking down over it. Then she shakes her head a bunch and mutters something and goes back to the chair. If you wait long enough, she will always do this. I think about the visit in terms of how many cycles I stay for. Once, I stayed for six cycles of the head-shaking. If I try to touch her, she says, no no no no no no nonononononononononono.

When that happens, I always cry. It is really stupid, and it breaks the rules because it is not something I am proud of. But, so far I have not been able to stop it.

My mom's gown is not always tied properly, so when she goes to look in the pool, her underwear is pretty visible. That is sometimes the occasion for the touching—I'm just trying to fix the gown so it covers her. She really doesn't like it, though.

I didn't want you to think I was trying to give her a hug or kiss her. I know that she doesn't want that—and I don't either, since she isn't actually anyone I know, and I'm not anyone that she knows.

FISH POND

The orderly came back and he must have noticed I was okay with him putting his hand on my shoulder, because he did it again, this time with both hands, one on each shoulder. So, I was sitting there and he was standing behind me sort of touching my shoulders. I leaned back a bit, which encouraged him more.

I said before that my mom doesn't really notice anything that happens. That's true. It's also true that the fish pond is behind a screen of trees on one side, and the back of another building with no windows on the other side. No one goes there, ever.

So, I didn't have many misgivings about it. I could tell that he was pretty happy about how things were going with his hands on me, and for the record—I don't get very much affection elsewhere, so I am a little starved. I was conscientious, I mean, when he started undoing my pants, I made sure we were going to do it safely, and he was like, yes, of course, and he showed me, and so—it felt really good. I can treat a person well. I really can, and he treated me really well. People aren't all horrible. They aren't. Sometimes you find a good one, at least for a while—even if it's just for twenty minutes or so.

While we were at it, I looked up and my mom had gotten out of her chair. She had come over toward the pool and was looking around in confusion as if she couldn't remember where to look. She came toward me and I met her eye, but there was no recognition, none. I must have shifted suddenly, because he shifted too. His hand moved over my breast and I shivered a little. That broke our gaze and I shut my eyes. When I looked back at my mom, she was over the pond, shaking her head, shaking her head, shaking her head.

DAY SIX

That Monday was my sixth detention, so I was done with
them for the time being. I finished writing the paper based
on *Russia Is Burning,* and it was much easier because it
turned out the school will loan me a computer to use while
I am there. I can't take it home—but I can check it out.
So, I typed the paper on that. It is a pretty bad computer.
Certainly, I don't look cool while using it, but I am a fast
typist, so it didn't take long.

Kennison came over and we had an argument about
citation. She had some idea about helping me, I guess.
But, I don't need help. She wanted me to do parenthetical
citation. I said footnotes are fine. She failed to present
a cogent argument about why her way is better. I said
footnotes allow for the author to comment on the source
immediately *at the point of use.* She basically threatened me
with more detention—but that was just because some of
the students laughed when I clowned her.

Lana was there again. Maybe she is my friend. We went to
a twenty-four-hour donut shop where her cousin works.
He gave us free donuts. She kissed him a little and that's
when I knew he wasn't her cousin. She said she calls him
that because she thinks it's funny. I thought to myself—this
is my kind of girl, and I said, you think that because it is
funny. It is funny.

MY DAD'S LIGHTER

We went outside the donut shop to smoke a cigarette and Hal, her "cousin," asked to use my dad's lighter, which I was holding in my hand (as usual). I gave it to him.

He did some zippo tricks with it and lit his cigarette. I did some too, so we have that in common now. He told Lana that I was cool, that it was cool with him if she brought me around now and then. It wasn't a creepy thing to say—it was more like, the three of us can talk without other people messing it up, so let's keep doing that.

He doesn't go to school. Hal thinks school is a waste, and I could not fucking agree more.

I want to describe my dad's lighter to you.

It is a zippo, so it is made up of several parts.

There is an outer shell, a metal case. That holds the parts together. The shell is rectangular, but it is curved at the edge, almost slightly beveled. The top of the case has a true curve across it. Even with all this curving that I'm describing, the main impression you get from the zippo is flatness. All the sides, even the top, they're all pretty flat. It is intensely comforting. Some lighters seem like they'll jump out of your hand. The zippo is the opposite of that. The tricks and things that you can do with it are evidence. The zippo likes to be in the hand—it isn't trying to flee the hand. You can pop it open, make it do a somersault—whatever you want. It isn't trying to escape to the ground.

That's the case. Inside the case, there is a sort of spring attachment that flips the top up or down. This spring attachment is connected to the body of the lighter. The body of the lighter consists of: the wick, the flint, the striking wheel, the cloth-like part that holds the fluid. Essentially, the zippo is always releasing gas. If you keep one in your pocket, your pocket will smell like gas (or it will smell like what they make gas smell like so you can smell it).

The outside of a zippo can look a number of different ways. Sometimes it will have a Vietnam kind of POW you are not forgotten thing going on. Sometimes it will have a USMC thing. Sometimes, just a skull. Some of them are mirrored. Others are matte silver. Some are dull black. Like other blue-collar things they will often feature gambling elements, like dice, cards, pool balls, or flags. My father's is matte black and has a white dot in the center. I haven't seen another like it. Years ago, I thought about asking him if he had done it himself, but I realized, and this was kind of a big deal for me to be smart enough at that point to realize something like this—I realized that I didn't want to know. I liked not knowing. So, I still don't know. The only thing that will make it clear is if one day I see another exactly like it. To be precise, that won't make it 100 percent clear. But, it would make it likely.

Other things that can vary about zippos:

1. Some are smaller—I don't know why. Maybe those are marketed to women, or to men with small pockets.

Often, people want to say that things are "for men" or "for women," but I think that many of these items just share the property that they can or can't fit into the shitty pockets women get. Of course, if girls were less focused on their appearance, maybe they would wear carpenter's pants and carry whatever they wanted. Who is to say? It is inarguable, though, whomever's fault it is, that having small pockets is terrible.

2. Some are looser or tighter in the way they snap open.

3. Some leak like crazy.

4. The inner cartridge on some slips around, so that when you go to shut the zippo, it doesn't shut properly. This was happening with my dad's, so I put a little sand into the case, and it is tighter now.

MY AUNT

was in the middle of beating me six times in a row in cribbage. They call it a skunking or something like that. I was getting skunked. That's when someone tapped on the door. I figured, it is the landlord, since no one else ever comes to the house. My aunt knows nobody. I know nobody. There isn't anything left to take. Why would someone come?

But, when I went to the door, Stephan was there.

Stephan, what are you doing here? How do you know where I live? It's eight o'clock. I said something like that to him.

He said it was on the emergency contact card we had to fill out that day. He got the pile of cards for a second and he has a photographic memory.

I thought to myself that this explained why he sometimes seemed smart and sometimes not. I didn't say that to him; maybe I should have. Sometimes people need to know what other people are thinking.

Mostly, though, I was just embarrassed about him seeing where I live, and then I was ashamed for feeling embarrassed about it, because it is a shallow thing to be embarrassed like that—and certainly not a way of behaving that I could feel proud about.

So, I said, come inside. You can meet my aunt.

Aunt, I said, this is Stephan. He is a convicted child molester. He wants us to know that he lives in our garden now.

My aunt laughed in a congenial way that put Stephan at his ease despite my awkward joke.

Do you go to school with Lucia? she asked.

He said he did.

She has a very foul mouth, don't you think? Sit down and have some tea with us, she said. We're just playing cribbage. Do you play?

Stephan took a gander at the room. I could see he was repulsed a little and when he looked at me, maybe he pitied me a little. I try not to be good at identifying pity in people's eyes. It is mostly better not to.

Anyway, he sat down, and my aunt explained the rules of V_I_C (veritably improved cribbage) to him, and then she beat us both really badly a few times and went to sleep in her chair.

Do you want to go for a walk?

Okay.

We went outside and walked for a while.

I heard what happened, he said.

About the pencil? It's nothing. He was an asshole.

Not that. Of course that's nothing. I mean—about your parents.

How did you hear about that.

Jay Lesso.

Oh. Jay, he's okay.

Yeah. Anyway—I'm sorry about that.

There is a really dirty canal that is near my aunt's place. We went to it and threw some paving stones into it.

Stephan told me that he was going to set a fire.

I said that I doubted it, he seemed kind of like a pussy to me.

Stephan repeated that he was going to set a big fire. He was planning it. He wondered if I would help him.

I said it is better to do those kinds of things by yourself.

He said, for this he would need a little help.

RUTTING

I think Stephan definitely wanted something else. A couple of times he seemed nervous as if he couldn't think of what he was trying to say, which is stupid, because he is smart enough to have a conversation without tripping up. He did this weird thing where he would take off his watch and put it back on. So, I knew.

It wouldn't be so bad. There's nothing objectively wrong with him. But, since he was someone I could talk to about setting fires, I figured—if you are a young woman, there are many people who want to do things to you that they enjoy doing to young women, so if someone is interesting for other purposes, it can be good to use them for those other purposes and avoid the things that anyone could do.

To be totally honest, and I like animals, it is just about rutting like animals. I ask you—is the best thing we're capable of just rutting like animals? We need to do it, yes, just so we don't get anxious, but for the rest? If someone says to me, Lucia, do you want to train to be a great spelunker so we can explore some unexplored part of Carlsbad Caverns, I mean—that is definitely more interesting. I say yes to that. I guess it's true also—you can do both kinds of things with the same person, but I haven't found anyone like that.

Before he left he showed me on his phone a video of some Pakistani soldiers beating a cow to death. It made me sad, but I also felt—how large the world is. There are many places and in some of them, people are beating cows to death for no reason. Meanwhile here we beat them to death out of sight and when they appear they are in neat cardboard packaging with tasty sauces.

I said that Darius once punished a river for drowning his favorite horse. Maybe this cow was being punished.

Stephan said he thought the cow was definitely being punished, but for what—who could say?

He asked me for my telephone number, but I don't have one—that was another embarrassing moment. He wrote his address on a piece of paper like it was 1990 and gave it to me. Jan is going to give a meeting at my house on Thursday, he said. My parents are away, so it's fine.

WORST THINGS

Whenever I have done the worst things that I have done—it is usually because I thought about doing something, and then I thought, Lucia, you shouldn't do that. Don't do that, Lucia. Then, I think, maybe I am just saying that to myself because I am afraid of doing it (the thing). What I fear most is being a person who is afraid to do things. So, at that point, I force myself to do the thing. Later on, it turns out one of two ways:

1. I was afraid to begin with, and it was good that I didn't let myself off the hook.

2. I wasn't afraid to begin with. I had some difficult-to-parse but correct misgivings about whatever it was, and when I go ahead and do it, things turn out badly, specifically because I was right and didn't pay attention to my feelings. This is when I do the worst things that I do. If someone else finds out about it, like my aunt, they say, why would you do that, with considerable astonishment. It's obvious you shouldn't do a thing like that.

We had to do one of those stupid occupational tests on Tuesday. First, there was a very long multiple choice. Then, there was a one-on-one interview with a counselor. In this case, I think they could have brought in a clown and it would have been more effective. At the very least, I would have enjoyed sitting with a clown for a while not talking. If neither of us talked for something like two hours, I would let the clown win, I would talk, out of sympathy. But, if he gave up early, I would be glad to claim victory over an undisciplined clown. What am I even talking about? There wasn't a clown—it was just a counselor, and the counselor asked me what my greatest weakness was. That's when I said that I was a coward at heart, but a recovering coward. She asked what did I mean. I said that I did everything I could to mitigate the effects of my cowardice. Why is that a weakness? she asked. I said it was because I then ended up doing absolutely inadvisable shit, like jumping off a pier onto a grain barge, or pulling a biker's ponytail at a hot-dog stand.

She asked what my greatest strength was. I said I was perspicacious. She pretended to have to go to the bathroom, but I could tell she was looking up *perspicacious* in her phone. That's okay. I would have said it differently, but I think it is a beautiful word. I guess it is my vanity (my aunt would say so), but I like to think it is true, I am perspicacious. One thing about perspicaciousness is that it doesn't have to be allied to traditional knowledge structures. It's just good clean insight. I aspire to be a perspicacious person, like a carpenter who knows which one of the beams is important.

The woman came back, and she had the results of my test with her. I was actually pretty eager to hear what it said. You might think these sorts of things are dumb, and of course I agree. However, they are mostly dumb when the results of the occupational test are someone else's results. Everyone finds their own results to be really interesting. Same with personality tests, all tests having to do with our paltry identities. What fools we are! I include myself in that.

Earlier, when I was waiting in the hall for my turn, Susan Dempsey came out, and she said she could be an architect, but also a performance coach. I don't know who thinks that is a job.

However that is—it made me curious. What weird thing might they tell me I can do?

Lucia, said the woman, your results in some parts are very good, and in others, well, you didn't even fill out all the questions.

I didn't think they could possibly test anything, I said.

This test is put together by very qualified people, said the counselor. It is certainly capable of testing any number of things. Your results, well, you shouldn't feel disappointed. The test doesn't ever show the upper limits of what you can do. You are always capable of much more than what others expect. It is very important for you to remember that.

I told her to cut out the bullshit. What did it tell me to be?

She handed me the piece of paper, which said my highest match was 69 percent with a career as a truck driver. I guess she thought I would be disappointed, but I thought that was great. Of course, I want a job where you work by yourself. The inside of those truck cabs are nice, too! Very comfortable. You can have a kick-ass dog with a bandanna. Sure, it is a bit jittery drinking twelve cups of coffee or popping pills to make a long-distance run through the night, but every job has its dangers.

She was looking at me very calmly. I don't understand it, really, she said. Your scores in these parts of the test are very high. It must be a mistake of some kind.

I don't think it's a mistake, I said. And you're definitely right—the test makers are very good.

Why do you say that? she asked.

Well, it's probably that—if someone scores more than a certain amount on the ability part, but then loses patience with the test and doesn't finish it, then that person is likely to hate having bosses, and being in office environments. So, such a person should be a truck driver or a park ranger or something like that. It's probably built into the algorithm for the test results.

She said she hadn't thought of that. Not finishing the test might be part of the test.

EMPTY LOT

Stephan came near me at lunch, which was surprising
because it meant other people would see that he had
talked to me. I figured that might be embarrassing for
him. It could be people would think he was trying to get
me to give it up, which guys are always proud about. If
a guy is a pariah, there is no reason to ever talk to him,
societally. But if a girl is a pariah, there is still one reason.
How fucked-up is that?

He said that his parents had come back. Apparently
his mom got food poisoning in Tangiers. I said that was
a lie. He said, yeah, it was because one of his dad's
patients was doing badly. They hadn't been in Tangiers
at all.

I said, I didn't think that Tangiers was actually a place.
It was something like Camelot, but for drugs and sex.
He started doing some misguided shit where he took
out his phone to show me Tangiers on a map. I know
Tangiers is real, I said. You are like four steps
behind.

He said we were going to meet at this empty lot, and he
told me where it was. Don't tell anyone where you're
going.

I told him I would go, but I wasn't sure. Meeting two or
three guys at an empty lot when no one knows you are
there?

I offered him some licorice, but he didn't want it. I guess he's one of those who don't like licorice. I think 75 percent of people hate it, but the other 25 adore it. What else is like that? Trampolines? Tanning salons? Parrots?

GYM

In gym class, we were playing volleyball. Yes, I know,
I told you I manage to avoid gym—but not always. I was
stuck in gym and we were playing volleyball.

That meant I had to wear gym clothes, which is awful. It
used to be everyone would wear ugly baggy clothes, but
now the pretty girls wear essentially spandex outfits. This
makes it awkward for people who don't feel like doing that.
So, I wear long basketball shorts and a black tank top. I do
that so people will know I am not wearing the same shirt
I wear during the day. It is no joke—it's a real thing. If I
wore a white tank top, they would think I didn't change,
and I would hear about it. Kids are jackals.

I mean, I like jackals more than kids, so the comparison
isn't fair.

The thing about this volleyball game, and the reason
I brought it up is—Clarence Eames, who is huge, and
really strong, spiked the ball on Jeanette Levy and broke
the hell out of her fingers. It was really really good,
because she is not a legitimate person and deserves
every bad thing.

She was crying and holding her fingers, and two of them
were obviously bent the wrong way. The gym teacher
tried to do some EMT business, but it failed and she just
screamed louder. Eventually the nurse came, and then
an ambulance. It was havoc, and I loved every second.

While the ambulance was coming, I had a fantasy in my mind. In the fantasy I am wearing a doctor's coat and just popping Jeanette's fingers in and out and she is screaming. I hold the fingers delicately in one hand and I hold her hand delicately in the other. I don't say anything, but my posture is like, *I am being reasonable. Calm down, Jeanette.*

That makes it even funnier (in the fantasy) when she can't stop screaming, because I am being a rock-solid medical professional—apart from the fact that I am, for reasons unknown, brutally reinjuring the finger as soon as I fix it.

When I was finished with this thought, it was time to go.

SATIE, ERIK

I saw a film the week that I moved in with my aunt. It was called *My Dinner with Andre.* Nobody really likes this movie. I like it a lot, and my aunt likes it, too. She says it is a good weather vane: if people like it, you might like them. It's possible, at least.

The movie has some Satie music in it, which is the first I had heard of this guy, Erik Satie. There are basically two things I like to listen to. One is a kind of headphone thing for concentrating. You put the earphones on and there is a tone that sounds sort of far away on one side. Then it goes away and after a while there is a tone on the other side. It is supposed to make you focus better than anything. I got completely addicted to it, and I used it for a long time until it broke, and then I found out they don't make it anymore. That was sad.

The other thing I like to listen to is Erik Satie. My aunt has a record of someone playing his stuff—and we listen to that. She wants to put it on when we are doing things. I refuse that. I want to sit in the chair and do nothing when I listen to this music.

By the way, I don't think that it is the greatest music. Bach is definitely better. Aretha Franklin is better. Everyone is better, I get it. There is a lot of really good music. I am not going to argue with you.

For me, though, I like to sit in the chair and listen to this Satie. I heard that he lived in a crappy little room in a boardinghouse, too, and was real lonely.

I think he was simultaneously feted and unappreciated.

But, that wasn't even what I was going to talk about—I wanted to tell you about this scene in the movie where the main character goes to a house party somewhere on Long Island, and has to dig a hole in the ground for his own grave, and then gets put in a coffin and buried and then taken back out and runs through the night naked to a shining white tent where some ascendant adoration and joy fill him entirely. I think he said it was like being born. When I heard about this, I felt like I was entirely ready to give up being who I am and ready to try being someone else. The trouble is—the someone else you are okay with being isn't anyone you know. So, who is it?

FIRE

Partway through second period, someone pulled the fire alarm. I figured it was just a prank. At Parkson, Will Scaffy used to get his older brother to call in bomb threats, and sometimes would pull the fire alarm himself until they got the ones that spray you to mark who did it.

But, this wasn't a prank at all. Someone had set fire to the music room. That is definitely not the room that I would have chosen, of all the terrible rooms at the school. Not that it mattered. I think just one or two chairs were set on fire.

But, we all got to go stand in the athletic fields, which was horrible, because I had to stand next to Jamie Anderson and her hair spray is like nerve gas. I almost fainted once, honestly. And, I'm not a fragile person.

The fire was not a bad one at all—but the principal decided to send everyone home, so the buses came early. I don't get a regular bus, so I just waited for Lana to see if she would show up, but she wasn't anywhere. This guy Rufus came up to me and asked if I knew who did it. I said why would I know. He said, he is asking everybody.

I watched him go off along the line of buses, and yeah, he was asking everybody. There are people, there really are, who think that they could be detectives if they wanted to. When I talk to these people I want to say, if you could be a PI or a detective, you would be. Being a detective is too exciting to not do it. If you aren't doing it, it's because you couldn't do it. So, stop telling me you could be a detective.

Detectives are a special case, though. Not everything is like that.

BEEKMAN

You remember I had the argument with Beekman. He's the
one who gave me the detention that led to six detentions.
Well, when I turned in my paper early, he was shocked.
Seems like he had me pegged as a dunce. I still don't think
he thought it would be good, though. He probably thought
I was trying to put one over on him by handing in a terrible
paper early.

I went into school, though, the next day, and Beekman
comes up to me at my locker and he is raving about my
paper. He says it is a really good paper. He says it is the best
one he's ever gotten. Okay. Take it easy, guy. It's a paper.

He goes off down the hall, and I figure it's the end of it,
but then O'Toole in math asks me why I can write such
good papers but don't do anything for him. He says I can't
leave class until I redo my last two tests, and he gives them
to me again. So, I do the tests, and fill in the answers this
time. I really wish Beekman hadn't blown the whistle
on me.

It gets worse, though. The rest of that day was fine, but
I guess Beekman talked to more people about the paper.
He wanted to put it up for some kind of award. It was just
too much.

So, last period, everyone comes down to the auditorium
to hear this speech that the principal gives about our
civic duty and how setting fires is evil, actually evil, and

that if anyone knows who did it, that person should come forward.

I think that they should, actually. If a person is a jackass who wants to burn up the music room, where delicate Mr. Alphonse who is from Spain or France and barely speaks English but is the only really kind one in the whole place, he sits there in the music room with crappy pictures of Mozart on the wall and tries to patiently teach people the fucking oboe, if they want to burn that room up, ahead of the rest of the godforsaken place, then yes—clap them in irons, I say. The order of things matters.

By the way, the principal was talking about evil, and I was thinking: how goddamned Manichaean this country is. Isn't it obvious that the world is a meaningless place where there is a faint impression you can leave on each other by being compassionate, but not more than that? And even awful things just pass away? I don't understand what evil is, and furthermore, I don't think he does. Our principal would love to take the occupational test from the guidance counselor and find out that he should be a principal. That would suit him right down to the ground.

I'm sorry for the digression. The point of all this is, after the auditorium speech—someone comes to the principal, another teacher, to talk about the paper that Beekman is blabbing about, my paper. So, the principal gets it in his head that I probably started the fire. He noticed that there was fire in the paper and a fire in the music room. He is basically a hero to himself.

MEETING

What does that mean? It means my aunt gets dragged
down after school, and I am sitting in the principal's office
again, this time with Mr. Alphonse across from me. He is
purposefully not looking at me. I think to myself—he really
thinks I did it. I was shocked.

I touch Alphonse's knee, and I say, mon professeur, je ne l'ai
pas fait.

(I asked my aunt how to say it.)

He smiles this really nice smile. It is like, I said something
to someone and for once they believe me.

The principal comes over. What did she say? Then, he and
Alphonse have some words off to the side and Alphonse
leaves. The old man didn't want to have anything to do
with it, since he knows I'm not the one. The principal is
showing Alphonse the paper, which he somehow has, but
Alphonse won't go with it. He says some shit in French and
leaves. My aunt laughs. What did he say? I ask. Something
about birds and donkeys, she says. I'll explain later.

The principal comes back and tries to be a tough guy with
us, but I point out that I was in a class at the time the fire
was set. He calls that teacher in over the loudspeaker,
and she hasn't left yet, luckily, because she is ninety years
old and slow. It takes her twenty minutes to get to the
office, but when she does, Ms. Cassidy tells him, yes,

Lucia Stanton was in Chemistry at that exact moment.
I give her a thumbs-up, but it only confuses her.

So, I'm like, too bad, I guess your little witch hunt didn't go
as planned. For which I immediately got a detention until
my aunt stuck up for me.

Or, I guess she did. They told me to leave the room, and
my aunt talked to him. When she came out, she said she
threatened to make a big deal out of me being accused if he
didn't can it. How could he go after a poor girl like me who
has done nothing?

My aunt, what a lady.

PAPER

I guess that meant I wasn't going to get an award for the paper. It's not like I worked that hard on it. Some of the other kids started asking me to write their papers for them. I said do your own work, weaklings. Actually, I didn't say that. I just said, no.

Beekman read some of it out loud to the class,

> Whatever this material means to the author,
> there is a dangerous implication. That implication
> is that the vengeful burning of one another's
> dwellings by these peasants is not political, and is
> not a thing that is performed with agency. In fact,
> the burning is a result of the ignorance forced upon
> the peasants by their masters, and by the imposition
> of a religious framework that fails to prepare them
> to weather the calamity of their daily lives. The
> people with agency in the situation have total
> agency, that is, the masters control completely what
> happens. When the peasants burn each other's
> huts, or even burn their own huts (by accident),
> the masters have chosen to permit the burning of
> the huts to occur. It is they who are guilty.

Everyone looked pretty bored while he read it, and I really wished that he would stop. At the end, he asked why it was good, which really made me turn bright red. I completely hid in my hood at the back of the class.

The first girl who raised her hand asked if she could get up to throw her gum out.

Beekman said yes, now—what was good about the paper?

Somebody said maybe it was good because I had read the book.

He said, that was important. He said he often got papers written by people who hadn't read the book. But, it wasn't that.

Someone else said something stupid, so Beekman was forced to come out and say it himself, which he should have done in the first place if he wanted it to get said.

He said, it was good because I read the book with an open but argumentative mind. He said the paper was at least good enough to be a college paper, whatever that means. I really wish that he hadn't said that part, but the first part was okay.

It is pretty stupid, how I felt. I felt that—I wished my aunt was there to hear it. She doesn't get to hear much that is positive about me. The landlord even told her I am a bad kid, which was rough. He is an old Ukrainian guy, and I thought he liked me.

The sad thing is, I can't even repeat this stuff about the paper because that would be boasting.

PSYCH VISIT

I guess this was the principal's revenge. Since he couldn't give me the detention without my aunt flogging him, he notified the psychologist that she should *check up on me.*

I want to see how you are settling in, she told me.

I sat down in her office and was immediately really unhappy. This is how it is—there are no chairs. I kid you not. There are two beanbags. She sits on a beanbag and you sit on the other, or, if you want, you both sit on the floor, I guess. Sometimes, she does this thing where she switches from the beanbag to the floor, like some kind of conciliatory gesture. The beanbag chairs are different colors, and I'm sure it means something to her which one you choose. Thinking that made me hesitant to sit before her, so I let her sit first, but I'm sure that means something too. She is really young, Ms. Kapleau, and extremely beautiful, which is why all the male teachers do boss stuff when she is in the hall, like clapping each other on the shoulder and leaning on things. Even the students do. I'm sure all the guys would like to fuck her. On this visit, she was wearing an inappropriate skirt. It was fine, as skirts go, but miniskirts and beanbag chairs are not a match made in heaven.

I told her that I was fine. I was going to try to make it for two more years and then be done. If I couldn't, I would leave before that, since I legally don't have to stay any longer.

What is keeping you here? she asked.

I said I didn't want to disappoint my aunt.

She asked me if I loved my aunt.

I didn't answer that. What bullshit—where they use whatever you say to make further questions.

Then, she asked if I was angry. I said that anyone who loves freedom should be angry. That shut her up.

We sat there for a while, and then she said she wanted to read me something. She got some shitty poem by Rumi and read it to me. *There is a candle in your heart . . .*

I laughed, and she asked me why I was laughing.

I said, you small-minded bitch, you think that is poetry? Of all Rumi's goddamned poems, you pick that one? Did you find it in some psych-nonsense anthology? That has to be his worst poem, and it isn't even translated well. How does it feel to wade around in life so hopelessly? You are just mired in shit. You're so limited.

I laughed some more. Of all the poems, that one.

She was looking at me in shock. I think she was actually speechless, so I gave her some more.

Whoever's calm and sensible is insane.

What?

I said, that's Rumi. Or didn't you know?

I didn't feel at all bad that I made her cry. After all, a school psychologist probably has to cry a lot in the first years of working at a school. There must be a great deal that they aren't ready for.

HOME

Well, I got in trouble for that. When I got home, I told my aunt the whole story, about the beanbags, the Rumi poem, everything. I did it because I felt like I had broken the rules. I wasn't proud of being mean to her. When I'm not proud of what I've done, I tell my aunt about it. I used to tell my dad. Now I tell my aunt.

I'm sure it gives her a picture of me that is pretty unflattering, since I tell her all the bad things, but none of the good ones.

She asked me if I thought that it was my job to improve the school psychologist.

I said, no.

She asked if I thought of myself as a person who goes around improving other people by showing them their shortcomings.

I said, no I wasn't that sort of person.

She said, it was puzzling then, why I would say that to the woman. Wasn't I trying to improve her? There was another explanation, she said. Maybe I just wanted to demonstrate to the woman that I was smarter than she was. Maybe I was showing off.

I said maybe it was that.

She said, if that was true, then it meant I must feel weak
and ashamed, if I need to demonstrate my intelligence,
rather than just having it.

She said that quietly, and then turned away to make
some tea.

Boy, did I feel awful.

My aunt, when she gives it to you, she really gives it to you.
When she brought the tea over she said it is possible my
comprehension was not of the really good sort, but just
a mean sort of proto-intelligence, and that was why I was
being mean. Maybe I was embarrassed about its quality
and magnitude, and that led me to go after these low-
hanging fruit.

I could see that the corner of her mouth was turning,
so I burst out laughing, and she laughed too. It was a
good joke.

BELL

Later that evening, we were sitting there and I could hear
a church bell from the Orthodox church around the corner.
My ear followed the sound there and back, there and back,
my eye trailing the distance to the church in the dark.
I asked my aunt if she was awake. She stirred in her chair
and said yes, she was. I said, how did you make it so long.
She asked what I meant. I said, there are so many years.
How can you be alone so long. She said she didn't know.

She pulled the blanket up onto herself and curled a little in
the chair. I could see she was thinking. She does this thing
where she cocks her head.

A person comes to the door. I ask: Who is at my door? What
do they say?

She asked me again, what do they say?

I said, I don't know. What.

She laughed.

They call to me from outside, It is you at the door, my love!

Wait, I remember, I said. I remember that. *It is thou,
beloved!*

Yes, she said. Jalal ad-Din Rumi. A person who was always
standing outside his own door.

EMPTY LOT

I went to the place, Fourth and Simonen, during the day, in order to check it out. Originally, I was just going to go at night to the actual meeting, but then I decided against it. I thought—why not go and look at what it is like and then you can have an idea about whether it is a terrible notion to show up there with some creeps and be potentially raped to death. This is what any right-thinking girl would say to herself.

Along Fourth there are a whole bunch of ramshackle houses. I guess they used to be brownstones. Now they are hovels. There are some places where you can give them a check and they give you 60 percent of the check in cash. There is a barbershop, no, there are three barbershops, and they are all open late, or so they say on the outside—you know, because everyone needs a haircut at one a.m.

I walked up and down the block and had some conversations that I won't repeat.

There was a little box someone had hammered to a telephone pole. It said, Community Library. There was a copy of a Dos Passos novel with the last chapter torn out (a nasty trick) as well as two Danielle Steel books and a shitty children's book about a unicorn. I know that because I read it standing there. The book is called *My Own Unicorn,* and it is about a girl who wants to have a unicorn, so her father buys her one, and then she is happy. I'm not kidding. That's the plot. The final picture is of a happy girl with her hand on the unicorn's mane.

My thought on that is—it wasn't a goddamned unicorn. The point of unicorns is you don't just get them. So the book isn't even bad, it's just invalid.

I had a thrift copy of Benjamin Franklin, some *Poor Richard's Almanac* stuff they put together. It was okay, but I had looked at it a little already, so I stuck it in there. Maybe someone will like it.

When I got down to Simonen, the neighborhood changed, if anything, for the worse. The *empty lot* as they called it was a housing project with a huge fence around it, half of it demolished, the other half decrepit. If I had to pick a place to murder someone, this would be it. I walked around the outside and it was enough to make you cry. It was very beautiful, too, though. I found a spot where I could climb the fence and I went in. It was really quiet in there.

The overgrown part was just a huge lot, maybe the size of a football field, maybe larger, I mean it stretched forever. All the crappy trees that grow when nothing else is growing were there, busting up through the concrete as far as the eye could see. All the walls, wherever they were bare, were covered in graffiti. There were piles of blankets or sleeping bags where people maybe had tried to live. I wandered across the lot. It took me ten minutes to cross it; I kept getting distracted by how alone I was—and how wonderful it felt. Eventually I got into the complex of buildings. There was a kind of driveway with window frames thrown down every fifteen feet. At the end of it was a beautiful courtyard. The windows from the buildings looked down into it and I got completely creeped out, but I couldn't run away. It was too far. Where would I run to? So, I found a place under a tree where the windows couldn't see me, and I sat and ate my lunch.

I was embarrassed to mention this earlier, but since I have said everything else, I might as well say this, too. My aunt makes me a lunch that I have when I go places (like school), since we can't afford to buy things. It is: a hard-boiled egg and a piece of bread and a carrot. The bread she makes herself and it is not good bread. Some people can make bread, some can't. My aunt is awful at it. I have eaten so much of this bread in the last year, I can't tell you. But, I am practically psychically compelled to eat it, because when I don't I have this grievous identification with her in my mind as she leans over the oven with her bad back taking the bread out. So, I have to eat it.

The good thing about that lunch is—it is over in about fifteen seconds. That leaves me more time for other things. Most people—their lunch takes them five minutes at least, sometimes ten or twenty, so they are lagging behind me in efficiency.

I have the licorice, too—which makes the shitty lunch bearable. When I run out of licorice, it gets bad.

You may be wondering whether I was brave enough to go into the buildings. I was not brave enough to go in. I had the thought that I would be a coward if I didn't go in. Then,

I looked at one of the places where the door was broken down. That's where I would go in, I thought to myself. Then, I thought, I am not going in there, no matter what. You can't make me. Then, I tried to make myself do it, and it didn't happen. So, I am that much of a coward, at least.

I went back to the lot, and found a nearer place where I could get out by climbing a wall on the inside. When I jumped down to the sidewalk, there were two guys playing dice in the shade right by me.

Shit, said one of them. What were you doing in there?

None of your business, I said, in a nice, play-along way, and he laughed.

I sat and talked to them for a while and watched them play cee-lo. I wanted to play too, but I didn't have any money. It's mostly luck, but it is slightly better to go first, so the trick is—you and your friends make sure the stranger has to go last. That way your money stays with your group. Eventually, then, you have all the stranger's money.

CEE-LO

You throw three dice and it is only something if you get:

111,222,333,444,555,666

or

any two that are the same and one of something else,
which counts as the something else, ie., 33,5 is a 5.

or

123 & 456.

The game is kind of rigged, and here's why: 1,2,3 is an
instant loss. You are removed from the game, but the game
continues for everyone else. Meanwhile, 4,5,6 is an instant
win. The game is over—bang. You get all the money.

So, the way to think of it—of whether it is fair—is to
consider, what if the game was just with one die and you
throw it—if you get a 1 a 2 or a 3 you win everything.
Let's imagine that is the game. Well, if that was the case,
then you would definitely not want to be last in a group
of people who are throwing the dice. Because then you
would have a 50 percent chance of losing your money
whenever someone else goes. And each of the five guys
who are ahead of you are going to go before you. If you
put in five dollars or ten dollars, which are common stakes,
you could lose as much as 25 or 50 dollars, without ever

getting to touch the dice! I grant you, in the actual game, that is uncommon, it would be 2 or 3 percent, I think, per roll of 456—but we are talking about the fairness—and over time, it ends up being pretty unfair.

So, you have to have enough money to suffer the loss that will happen before you get to go, just to make sure you have money to put in the pot for your turn, and then you'd better hope you have at least average good fortune when you do get to go first.

If it truly rotates and everyone gets to go first the same number of times, well, fine. But, people often get tricked out of going first because the dice game will move, people come and go. I have seen it happen. Also, people will often leave right after having gotten to go first, which is a creep move. If the players in the game keep coming and going— and there are a lot of fresh faces, and those people are getting to go first when they arrive for reasons you can't fathom, well, watch out! Basically the same trick is that they will change the bet when your turn comes around— so the time when you go first is a short-bet, and the rest of the times, the bet is large. The way they do this con is they let you go first, and everyone throws a dollar down. Then when that turn is through, they up the bet to five or ten.

One other trick they will do is when it is about to be your turn someone will throw the dice so that one die gets lost. Then the game is off until another die is found, and at that point there is a new order, and you are at the back of the line again. What bullshit! And if you try to argue, you could even get beaten up—or worse, some of these guys are charismatic. They'll just talk real sweet and make you seem like an asshole for trying to be some kind of stickler. But everyone knows what is actually going on.

There is a different version that is slightly more fair that involves the dice-throwing player being "the bank." Then, the rest match his/her bet. People will play that version if they play for a lot of money. I have only seen it once.

And as I was saying at the beginning, even if things are fair—you can be in big trouble when it is you versus a group of people who are friends. This is because they exist as a sort of big bank that preserves itself. Whereas, when you run out of money, you have to stop playing. You stop playing because they have your money and you have no money. They never have to stop playing because it simply won't happen (unless you are really lucky) that you win all of the money that they have in common.

Essentially, if you are going to weather bad runs of luck, you need to have enough money to never stop playing.

Enough about cee-lo. I'm sorry to talk so much about it—but I really like thinking about games. My aunt would definitely come up with some better rules if she were a dice player.

PAMPHLET

A few days before, at school, Stephan had given me a full copy of the arson pamphlet that he got when he went to somebody's house. I imagine he must have gone and photocopied it himself, which is ridiculous. He had to be really stuck on me to photocopy a whole pamphlet for no reason. I didn't even thank him. Sometimes when people get to be too nice, you end up not thanking them, because you are completely tired of saying thank you. Then they become more and more hangdog and you want to thank them even less.

The pamphlet was a bit long-winded. It was written by one of these anarchist types who want to prove that they could be university professors if they felt like it. He is imagining a cadre of university professors tearing his bullshit pamphlet up, and he wants to make sure that whatever grounds they have for tearing it up, it will damned well not be because the thing isn't *smart* and *awesomely argued on their terms.* Which is worse than nonsense. If it is a pamphlet about anarchism or setting fires it should be practical.

I will give you a breakdown of some of the material.

The pamphlet had an introduction. The introduction said that all over the United States, the lower class is fed up with being used. Okay.

Next, it said that the response to that is: people forming groups, syndicates, with the intention of burning down property. What cannot be shared should be destroyed. That's what he says. The organization of these groups varies from place to place, but it really doesn't matter how the organization is handled, or even if there is any, because the whole thing is just people burning things, so you don't need an organization in the first place.

As far as I can tell, the clubs are just there to be clubs, same as any club ever. You get to be around like-minded people and have a nice time.

Then he gets into how even children are joining in to this mayhem, and there are Arson Clubs in high schools. He quotes the record of one boy who was in elementary school. Apparently he burned down a train station in Ohio.

I found some of this doubtful, because I had never heard of any of it, and wouldn't I have? But then he addresses that, too, by saying much of it is suppressed.

So, that's the introduction. The first chapter is a history of arson, and talks about how it is mostly *on the record* in terms of insurance. People burn things to get money for the things that were burned. Then they pretend there was more there than was there and get money for the things that weren't even there to begin with! He talks about how people even existed once called *insurance adjusters* who would flock to burning buildings (in the 1920s) to offer their services. They would interact with the insurance company for you and juice up your claim, and for that they would take a percentage. Talk about living off your wits—what creeps. Not that it matters to take money from insurance companies.

The next chapter is about the ethics of arson. It points out that arson is a crime for which you can be murdered by the state. Or executed, as they like to put it. You burn something big down and if someone is inside and they die then you die. I think that is the logic.

In the past people who wanted to destroy property, like the Weathermen, for instance, tried to make sure no one was there. This is a kind of ethical version. The new way, he says, is a new ethic. What is it?

It is: the manner of exertion of the will of the ruling class is such that they do not appear responsible for the vast cruelties they inflict. Each wealthy person can cruise about seemingly innocent, despite in fact being a linchpin in a system that demoralizes and brutalizes the majority of living people. Yet when someone battles back, that person acts as part of a small machinery—the machinery of his/her individual action—and thus appears guilty. The rich, on the basis of their larger machinery of violent action, can disconnect themselves from the violence of their class warfare. The poor cannot—since they must be their own mechanisms for action.

On the basis of this, he says, we need a new morality. That morality is, if you are a person who owns a great number of things, if you are a person who uses the reins of power to manipulate others, then you forfeit your right to be treated like a person (that is, you are intrinsically connected to the murder you have *impersonally* done—and will be treated the way the state treats murderers).

There will be two classes of people: those who act in a small, meager way, or a small, meager, compassionate way, and those who live off them. The latter do not get to have the consideration that has historically been afforded to human beings under human moral law.

The crucial thing about this morality is that it enables poor people to more easily burn the machinery of the rich—as they don't have to worry about the rich people being inside the buildings that they burn. That in turn makes it safer for the poor to strike back, as they don't have to adopt extravagant measures of safety.

There is a section about arson in which you intend to not be caught, and then there is a section about arson in which you do intend to be caught. Why would you want to be caught? He says this is one of the best ways to broadcast *our methods* and *our rationale* to other people, although presumably the media will prevent such a thing from happening, for the most part.

I thought about this, and about the pamphlet that I would write. Mine would be more like:

HOW TO SET A FIRE AND WHY

And it would say all kinds of wonderful stuff about the joys of setting fires. There is definitely a lot to say about that. It would also present a more compelling moral argument. I think I could do that. Maybe there would even be inspiring verses about setting fires that people could memorize. If the technique parts—how to set a fire—were in verse, then people could memorize them more easily, and then they wouldn't forget, even under duress!

I made a note to work on my own fire pamphlet, since I found this one to be lacking. Still, there was plenty in it that I didn't know.

JESSE BALL

PAMPHLET three

The pamphlet got to the good part eventually, which was a breakdown of methods.

As I mentioned, those methods could be divided into two categories, concealed methods and bald methods. The concealed methods attempt to use only things that are present in the place of conflagration in order to burn the place of conflagration. That way no one can say how it happened. The bald methods use other materials in order to ensure a successful fire (it is by no means easy to set fire to a building). Those materials will often be discovered after the fact, and the arson will be discovered.

Having arson discovered is not so bad for us. We, the arsonists, are not trying to get money from insurance companies. In fact, the more arson that is discovered, the more we can feel the growth of our fraternity (this is what he says).

I say he, but really the pamphlet could as easily have been written by a woman. Certainly, the name on it is a man's name. But, a woman could well choose to write the pamphlet under a pseudonym. I'm sure men would prefer to read an arson pamphlet by a man.

Anyway, I am fed up with telling you about this arson pamphlet. I will just stick in my own pamphlet a bit later on. You have that to look forward to.

INVITATION

When I got home from my expedition, my aunt said
that someone had called for me. I prefer to be the one to
answer calls like that, because then it seems like I have
an actual phone, rather than a home telephone. I think my
aunt is the only person in the world who still has a home
telephone. Anyway—Lana called to invite me to a party.
My aunt said she was real cordial on the phone. I said,
Lana is a vicious slut. My aunt said she would never have
known.

About this invitation: I won't even try to pretend that
it isn't a big deal. I have only been to a few parties, and
it was usually with asshole guys who took me there to
give me liquor. I am a sort of escape artist, though—
so don't worry, I almost always manage to extricate
myself gracefully, even if sometimes I am a bit
wobbly.

Lana and her friend Ree came to get me. They pulled
up in front driving some kind of old convertible (it was
red and gorgeous). I was sitting on the stoop—which
annoys our landlord to no end.

Nice house, Ree said. Get in.

Lana leaned her head back to look at me through the seats.
She narrowed her eyes:

Do you ever wear different clothes?

No, I said. I am not a wardrobe kind of person.

Got it.

She peeled out, and my heart basically took off into the fucking sky.

THE PIER

The party was at this house that is called *the pier*. That's
what Ree told me. She did this cool thing where she
climbed over the seat and sat in the back with me to talk as
we drove. Ree is Asian, I think probably Korean, and also
part Indian, which is weird, I mean, uncommon. I have
never heard of this combination, but she is really hot, so—
nice for her. She started telling me about the place and put
her elbow on my shoulder like someone in a movie. It
killed me.

The pier is a house that has a backyard that used to
be a water park. So, it is maybe three acres (it was a shitty
water park). There is no water, and all the pools and slides
are empty, but it is a great place to hang out. When she
told me this, I almost didn't believe her. It sounded too
good.

But, when we got there, it was absolutely true. It is on
the edge of the city, so there are farm fields and woods
and such around. Ree said there is actually a sanitation
plant over the hill, which is what put the water park out
of business.

There were maybe a hundred people there already—
for which the host, a guy in his forties with no shirt on,
apologized. *It'll heat up, don't worry.*

I hate when people say that kind of thing. He knew Lana
and Ree and gave them hugs. I did not do that, although

he moved to sort of make it happen. I gave him a good handshake.

Get yourself some drinks, he said. Mona'll be back soon with a truck full of fireworks.

Mona, Ree told me, is that guy's (Jim's) girlfriend. She is maybe thirty and an awesome singer. What kind of singer, I asked. Not like that, said Ree. She is an opera singer.

Shit.

I decided I would try to get her to sing for me later on.

JARED

A couple of hours later, Lana and I were sitting at the top of a slide and this real dumb guy named Jared, who is supposedly in a famous law school, is telling me how Lewis Carroll was a pedophile. I can only take so much of that, you know. I mean, honestly.

From the spot where I was sitting I could see the whole water park laid out beneath me—or I would have been able to in daylight. Now, it looked a bit like a diorama, or a structure that you're in, but that you understand from above—like in a dream.

Jared was being so annoying I finished my drink, and that drink was supposed to last me a good hour. So, I turned against him.

He was starting to say some more, and I had to get away. If Lana wants to talk to him—fine.

I got up, and he had to move to let me go back up the slide to go down the ladder.

Be easy, be easy, I told myself, but then I decided not to. I turned to him:

You aren't a pedophile because you like to take pictures of naked children. Maybe it's weird. Yeah, it is. Maybe that's true. But, I bet being eight and naked and having a chat with Dodgson is better than 98 percent of the activities you could get to do, ever.

He looked shocked.

Lana laughed.

You would have let him put it in, eh? Eight-year-old Lucia
would be into that?

Lana. You know what I mean.

I kept going toward the ladder, but remembered the rest
of what I had to say to the lawyer-guy.

And for the record, it is Alice Liddell, not Little.
Some—people—.

My speech was ruined by the fact that I almost tripped
and fell, but I caught the mouth of the slide, and got to the
ladder okay. The guy said something, and I could hear Lana
saying to him,

Oh, no, she just hates poseurs. You're not a poseur, are you?

That actually almost made me fall. I don't want you to
think that this whole ladder and slide business was a piece
of cake. The ladder was maybe thirty feet long, and many
of the rungs were broken. Just getting up there in the first
place was not something everyone could do. In fact, I had
been surprised to find this Jared individual there when we
got to the top.

On the way down the ladder I remembered I had to go to
the bathroom, which meant trying to remember where the

bathroom was. That meant remembering that there were four different ones (it was a water park after all). Ree was in line outside one smoking a cigarette. She passed it to me and lit herself another, like we had been doing that kind of thing forever. When the bathroom opened up, she said, in you go, and we went in together.

That made me a little nervous, because I didn't want to mess up how cool we were being with each other, but we got inside and she just pulled her dress up and started pissing in the toilet, still smoking away on her cigarette.

I looked at myself in the mirror. It was cracked as hell and there was a naked bulb blinking on and off right above it. I messed around with my hood a bit and stuck my chin out.

Hold it there, she said. Let me get a picture of you. Hold on.

She was still pissing and smoking a cigarette, and she pulled her phone out of I don't know where. I love this photograph, she said. You are so beautiful. Grow old and die right now and I'll play piano at your funeral.

DOGS

A guy named Walt who had three pit bulls with him gave
me a ride home in his Wagoneer sometime around dawn.
He was pretty old, and his dogs were all sweet as fuck. If
you like dogs, he said, you should sit in the back. They will
sit all over you. So, I did that. I was thinking, I like these
dogs, and, these dogs can actually predate on me if they
choose to. One of them, Mona, was 115 pounds. How heavy
do you think she is, Walt asked me. I said, she is definitely
heavier than I am.

Mona had an awesome white patch on her face. She kept
doing the dog thing of knocking the head into me and
leaning against me to try to provoke some petting. In her
case, though, it is not really a question. You will pet her
or she will eat you.

Walt dropped me at the corner and Mona gave a little wail
when I got out. The other two dogs didn't care as much. She
never likes anyone, Walt said, which is what dog owners
always say. Does everyone believe it? I usually do.

AUNT

My aunt was awake when I came in, or I thought she was, but she was kind of frozen in her chair. It is hard for me to describe it, but her body was really weird and stuck. In my head, I heard a voice I hadn't heard before, some voice of knowledge say in a slow clear way, *she has had a stroke.* I think it was probably just my own voice, but I was so far away at that point, I couldn't even recognize it.

The ambulance came, and they told me I couldn't ride in it. They carried her out of the house, which was strange— having these men I don't know inside our house—and then they wouldn't let me get into the ambulance. You're drunk, they said. Sober up. I tried to insist, but they said no, and gave me the address of the hospital. One of them led me away from the ambulance a short distance while the other shut the door, so I couldn't even jump in.

I don't know why they wouldn't let me go along with her, but it was awful.

Essentially, ten seconds passed, and I was standing on the street, it was six a.m. and the ambulance was gone. Some people who had been woken up by the sirens were looking at me out their windows. I felt like a real fuckup.

It happened so fast that I had the thought—*just jump in the ambulance,* after the ambulance was gone. Then it turned a corner in my head and became, *why didn't you jump in the ambulance?*

Then, I felt even worse waiting for the bus, because I stopped being drunk and I stopped being high, and I was just hungry and the bus took forever to come. When it did, it got me partway. I had to wait for another bus. That got me to the hospital.

One thing about hospitals is—it isn't always clear how to get into them. You can walk around the outside a long way looking for the entrance, and then when you find it there are thirty-foot letters that say, Emergency, or Outpatient.

I wasn't sure if I should go into the emergency room, but I did, and then I had to wait to talk to the nurse because there were people truly bleeding who were on line in front of me. A little girl was throwing up into her mom's purse. I'm not kidding. The mom was holding the purse open, and the kid was throwing up into it.

Forty-five minutes later, when I managed to speak to someone, I got hassled about not having any identification, and I solved that by crying.

At that point, there was nothing they could do but take me to her, so they did.

AUNT two

Before we get to what happened when I went to my aunt's room:

a fact:

my aunt wrote a book. I didn't know that she had done that until after she was in the hospital because my aunt is almost always in the house when I am in the house and so I never really get to poke around the way you do when you are alone. And that's the poking that really counts, because inevitably you find things that lead to other things, and next thing you know you have emptied out someone else's drawers and are looking at notes they wrote to people who are long dead.

At the bottom of one of the drawers was a book called *Falstaff, the Proper English Gentleman: An Indictment of Culture* by Lucy Stanton, D.Phil.

This isn't really my type of book, so I only looked at it for a little while. I think it is about things that were important to people once, but not really anymore. By the way, it has nothing to do with Shakespeare, if that much wasn't already obvious.

I also found a letter from her husband. It is on the inside of a paper airplane, which I guess makes sense since they were essentially children together (he died when she was nineteen). The paper airplane is inside of an envelope, some kind of military envelope. I guess he was overseas when he sent it to her, which is weird, because he didn't die in the army, so he must have been there before he died.

It seems there was a period when they were apart—he was in the army and she was still in school. He would write her letters, she would do the same. This letter was a paper airplane that was inside an envelope. I imagine she took it out and it must have been pretty exciting. No one has ever sent me a letter, certainly not with a sweet paper airplane in it.

So, the letter says on the outside:

just in case the letter doesn't get all the way to you, I gave it some wings so it could fly the rest of the way.

Which is pretty terrible, but is the kind of thing a guy might write to his sweetheart when he is sitting in a barracks somewhere.

The letter on the inside is just him going on about how pretty she is and how much he misses her, and about the books that she sent him, which he read, and all the things they will do when he gets back. He lists a ton of plans they must have made, and I think it is really sad, because I know for a fact that he died early in that next year, so they must never have gotten to do most of those things.

Now,

when I was crying at the hospital, they took me up to her room, and I thought, definitely she isn't in there, because

I could see the bed and it looked empty, but when we got over to it, I could see she was there. With the hospital clothes she just looked really small. She was asleep and the nurse gave a sign that meant—don't wake your goddamned aunt because she almost died. The nurse was a really fat Puerto Rican guy. We went out into the hall and he turned out to be one of these nurses who knows everything. He even asked me stuff about what my plans for the week were and gave me good advice about not having a guardian around.

Regarding my aunt, he said—she had a stroke. Now, she is asleep. Her condition is stable. We don't know any more than that yet. There will be a bunch of tests.

If her condition is stable, I said, doesn't that mean you'll just release her? We don't have any money and we have no insurance.

He said somehow the no money no insurance thing wasn't known at the hospital yet, so I should shut up and see how much care she could get before it got cut off. I gave him an I'll-keep-mum-soldier-salute, kissed my aunt on the cheek, and headed to the elevator. While I was waiting there, he came and found me. He had a sheet that listed visiting hours, phone numbers, other data.

I dropped the paper and knelt to pick it up. When I got to my feet, he was looking back at me.

She might be really changed, he said. Think about it.

LUCIA SERIES

When I was sitting at home by myself, I decided to write a series of descriptions for my aunt. I could bring them in to her at the hospital so she would feel like she knew what was going on outside.

Maybe one would be about the garden, one would be about the house. One could be about my school, one about buses, because I really like them. I don't know, I kept thinking it was a dumb idea, but it stuck. I was sort of pretending that I would be able to see my aunt again, that I would go back to the hospital and she would be there in her body. But, obviously, there was no guarantee of that. My mom is an example of this—one day she left her body and I have never seen her again.

When I say that, I don't mean that she actually went somewhere else. What I mean is: the shitty little cells that cluster together to muster up in sum total the person I used to know are now clustering in some inferior way and the person I know cannot ever be found.

My mother isn't even really in my memory—because it constantly erodes. Everything is falling apart all the time.

People love to say it to you like it counts:

Oh, Lucia, she will live on in your memory.

Sometimes they'll even touch your arm at the same time like they've earned it by saying something poignant.

The whole thing about people living on in memory is a crock of shit. The best you can do is try to remember what you can, and include the memories in your routines. But, sometimes that makes the real memories fade faster.

We're just running down a fucking slope carrying these little flags, and one by one we get shot and we slump and our little flags are in the mud and no one picks them up. No one is going to keep running with your flag. Lucia, no one cares about your flag. I tell myself that. When you fall down it's over.

TELEPHONE

I called the school and told them I was spending the day
at the hospital. Immediately on hanging up the phone I
realized this was a big mistake. If my aunt dies and the
school knows, and now they know, then it could mean
some kind of institutional business. I mean, they can't send
me away anywhere, I don't think so, but—better to keep
it all quiet as long as possible, and here I go calling them
when I don't need to.

Why not just fail to show up on Monday, and then on
Tuesday bring a forged note? I think I called because I
wanted to tell somebody what had happened. The sad little
individual that I am wanted to hear somebody feel bad
about how bad it was for me and wanted to hear a voice
wish me well. That's what happened. The lady at the main
office, who I hate, she is really terrible (I see her talking on
her cell phone outside the school entrance when I eat lunch
there by myself sometimes—and she is just abominable),
this very lady is the one who answers the phone (of course
she is, she is the receptionist), and she listens to my pathetic
retelling of my aunt's stroke, which I feel bad about even as
I do it, and she says, essentially, oh my little bird, you poor
dear, oh you frail thing, of course don't come to school.
I'll let everyone know.

It didn't make me feel any better—in fact, I felt a bit worse,
because she thought she had hung up the phone, and
maybe a second later I heard her talking to someone else
in the office about how she was going on break and could
someone replace the toilet paper in the office toilet for once.

AUNT

I went to see my aunt and she was talking. First thing,
I said maybe you should pretend to be in a coma so they
can't release you.

She said, it was fine. Someone from the soup kitchen, a
woman my aunt has never liked, came to visit and is paying
for all her care. She showed me a card the woman brought.
It had a Jesus face on it (Shroud of Turin style). I guess she
has a ton of money stuffed in a mattress or something,
and is really kind. My aunt was kind of sheepish about it,
because she thinks she is a good judge of people. Let me
tell you—no one is a good judge of people.

I said, now you have to live.

Why?

You have to live so you can get the chance to be nice to her.

Right, my aunt said. I can live a little longer.

I asked her how long she was going to be there for. She said
a week at least, because they had been finding some other
things that were wrong with her. That's the trouble with
the hospital—they find all the things that have been killing
you forever, and that you are okay with, you're okay with
those things slowly killing you, but then they find them and
get rid of them, and then other things replace the things
you were fine with, and you are *not fine,* not fine at all with

the new things, and so you die, slowly, in utter misery, just the way you would have before, only before you were pretty okay with the manner of it, but now you're not.

I told her my idea about writing some descriptions for her. She said she liked that idea, but I should make sure not to ham it up. She wanted good clean descriptions, no sentimentality. I was a bit offended, I said, who died and made you king, of course I won't fucking write you sentimental descriptions just because you had a stroke and shat yourself.

It isn't anyone's fault what they do at a time like that, my aunt said. The ambulance ride was really bumpy.

I asked her did she really shit herself and she said no.

LUCIA SERIES

I got out my notebook and practiced doing typography.
I realize it isn't real typography. It is just me drawing some
letters, but I tried hard and made it look pretty good.

I figure I will assemble it all and have it actually printed up
on cardstock and give it to my aunt. She likes real books.

The cover proof I made looked like this:

LUCIA
SERIES
1–10

1 GARDEN

The garden is a pathetic little plot of nothing. Someone once laid stone down to serve as a walkway, but the stone has long ago cracked apart until now it must always fail at its mission, which is to give a person a place to put her feet when she walks there.

The beds, which are raised, or are supposed to be raised, are often broken open on one side or the other, that is, the wood boxes are broken, and the earth has crumbled out and fallen, so the raised beds slump here and there to the ground, crowding or occluding the path.

The choice of plants has no overall rationale. Essentially, the person who plants a plant in this garden does not think about any of the other plants when she does it, she thinks only of the plant she is planting and whether she likes it.

To say that this gives the garden a *motley* appearance would be a pretty far-fetched compliment. In fact, it makes it not seem very much like a garden.

The garden may be seen from the windows of the converted garage. It may be seen from the bench that abuts the garden just before the converted garage. It may be seen from the space where an automobile once parked next to the converted garage. It may also be seen from any of the twenty windows of the huge house that stands before the garden. Most of those windows are covered with curtains and blinds, however, so in reality, no one ever looks out of them, and that is partly because the landlord lives in only a few rooms of the house and has the rest shut up *to preserve it,* as if that were a thing.

A person can use the garden by: reading in the garden, playing an instrument in the garden if she has a musical instrument, singing in the garden, sitting in the garden, speaking to a friend in the garden, if she has a friend and that friend is dear enough to be permitted to see the garden, or walking in the garden. Walking in the garden is not much of a walk because the garden is fairly small.

Certainly, you can't call the garden *the gardens* as some people do (regarding their own large garden).

The garden is poorly kept. The garden is full of dead things. The garden does not get as much sun as it should. When you are in the garden you can still occasionally hear noise from the street. The garden is inexpert. It appears abandoned.

In sum: the garden has excellent character, and it knows all the right people.

2   THE BUS

The person is rare who enjoys taking the city bus. Yet, here she is. Here I stand before you, an actual enjoyer of city buses.

The reason is this: for a person who rarely has privacy, the city bus gives you a place that can't be taken from you—a place where you can sit and read or write, or if you are lucky listen to music on headphones, and not be bothered (too much). For someone who already has the book she wants to read, it is like a library on wheels.

The bus has an awful smell. The seats of the bus are vile and you always feel that you are going to catch ill from touching them. The people who ride the bus collectively smell worse than other people. The bus drivers will not always treat you nicely, though sometimes they appear to be absolute saints.

The back of the bus, contrary to popular opinion, is not the best place to be. It is far better to be near the front. Why? People who vomit and leak tend to go to the back. It is also possible to have people steal your shit while you are on the bus and this happens more often at the back.

When not to ride the bus—

do not ride the bus at rush hour because you will have to stand. Standing on a bus is not an experience I am prepared to defend. Late at night is the best time.

I once took a bus and the driver forgot he was a bus driver. He drove the bus somewhere he wasn't supposed to and didn't stop at the bus stops after a while. Finally someone confronted him. He said he had a lot on his mind, and to give him a break. I thought this was a legitimate defense.

One of the other riders called him a fucko, and the others agreed, which has to be the first time anyone has gotten a consensus with the word *fucko*.

3   ABANDONED WATER PARK

This is a place you have never gone to, and to which you never shall go. It is full of young people who are extremely drunk. I understand that your understanding of what it is to be young is different from what I think it is, probably more accurate, and also full of supporting identifiers that I cannot recognize. Still, picture this abandoned water park as being crammed to the gills with the stuff of life.

That it is abandoned means: it is not being used against you, like the rest of the city.

That it is full of people who are drunk means: you can understand what they are doing and why and you don't have to fear them as much as when you wonder what they want. You can wander through the water park observing things.

The water park has lots of construction area lightbulbs in plastic cages strung on lines all through it. The man who lives there thought of this as a cheap way to make things nice for people.

Many of the ways to go from one place to another in the water park are broken. Walkways are broken. Ladders are broken. Slides are broken. Bridges are broken. There are fences where you wouldn't think they would be. It is a bit of a maze.

If you want to be able to get around the abandoned water park without help, you need to get there when you are still sober, and you need to get there when it is still light.

The best situation at the water park is to have some friends with you and to go away from them and then to hunt for them and find them and then to go away from them and then to hunt for them and find them. In the meantime, you meet other people, many of whom are not worth talking to, but some of whom are okay.

Sometimes you are in the *going away from them* part of the instructions, and then you are surprised because you have fallen out of sync and one of your friends comes and hunts for you and finds you, and as it turns out, that is just as good.

You should have: licorice, a cup, a flashlight, a notebook, and a screwdriver.

You must never under any circumstances fall asleep in some far-off part of the abandoned water park. If you are tired, you should find the opera singer who (apparently) sings all the time during the day at the abandoned water park, and ask her if you can lie down on their couch.

Really, though, if you are tired, you should go home. The abandoned water park is the sort of place that attracts rather decent people, so it is likely someone will take you where you need to go.

That's enough of my descriptions for now. I'll put some more in later.

How things stand at this point if you haven't been paying attention:

I go to Whistler High School; everyone hates me, except Lana and maybe Stephan (and some other people whose response to being school-victims is to try to uselessly band together). I like Lana.

My mom is in a mental hospital. My aunt is in a real hospital.

I spend most of my time thinking about joining the Arson Club, which I will do, and I am writing a pamphlet about setting fires. I have not actually set any fires yet, but I can do a better pamphlet about it anyway than some people who (maybe) have.

So—

Jan canceled the meeting with me and Stephan. He
did this by just not going, which is the best way to
cancel an appointment, I have found. That means
Stephan went there alone and wandered around like
a moron for two hours looking for us.

The other day, I went there and wandered around
happily knowing I wasn't looking for anyone. But
Stephan, he went and wandered around in the dark
like a moron feeling he'd been tricked. That's a
comparison of our two experiences. I am not being
superior—if our positions had been switched, I would
be the one scrabbling around in the dark like a mole rat.
Or, actually, not like a mole rat. Mole rats are really
great at being in the dark. They are totally content
there. It is hard not to feel some fondness for
them.

Stephan was a little mad that I hadn't gone, and he
was being a bitch about it. So, I told him about my aunt's
stroke, and my aunt's stroke trumped his irritation.
He apologized immediately. I guess he has pretty good
manners.

He said he called Jan and we would meet in two
days. I said okay. He said, did I want to go today to
burn something. I said, I was really busy, but I would
go to the other meeting, so he should make sure to go
to that.

He said, of course he was going to fucking go to that. That was his meeting that he got me invited to. I said, fine, if you think so.

That's how things are with Stephan. He doesn't reassess things often enough. I think he is still pretty immature.

ENGLISH

In English class, the teacher, VanDuyn, announced that we were going to do a creative writing module. Someone asked what that was. The teacher said he was going to teach us to share our thoughts and ideas in fiction. A bunch of the kids got really stressed out, I guess because they think that their thoughts and ideas are completely worthless. Ordinarily, I would stick to the party line and say that everyone has useful stuff to say, but this group of kids, I don't know. I think probably they were right to be stressed out.

So, VanDuyn had everybody take out their laptops. If you don't have a laptop, he gives you a block of paper. One girl, Maya, has no laptop because she has broken three of the school laptops. She takes them to the fourth-floor bathroom and throws them out the window. No one knows why she does it, but when she does she gets a lot of credit from everyone. It is really funny. She pretends it is an accident each time, but she still gets in trouble. So, Maya and I got blocks of paper, is what I'm saying, and everyone else had a computer.

VanDuyn read to us from an essay by some Pulitzer Prize–winning author. He said, to enter the sweet land of fiction, think about something outside of yourself. Then imagine yourself inside the thing. Then that is a story.

I have no intention of entering the sweet land of fiction, wherever that is.

We worked on the stories for three days in English class. On the third day, we had to give ours to the person next to us to read. I gave mine to Grace, and Grace gave me her laptop with the story open on it.

It's not really done, she said.

Mine is, I think.

Grace's story is called DOLPHIN FRENZY.

It is about a dolphin named Reno who wants to go to the big city. I'm not kidding. You can't make this stuff up. The problem with Grace's story is that after the first page, on which we get a bunch of Reno's thoughts, most of which are small-town thoughts and thoughts about swimming, Grace runs out of steam. She starts just putting in facts about dolphins. I don't want to accuse anyone of anything, but the language changes a little, so it seems like maybe she copied the quotes from somewhere. Here's a sample:

Reno woke up late and his mom was already setting the breakfast table. He took off the sheet and got up and brushed his teeth. Got to run, Mom, he said, and got just to the bus in time. Some common dolphins are: the common dolphin, Fraser dolphin, Clymene dolphin, Pacific white-sided dolphin, and others. New dolphin species are discovered every day. If you can have a curved dorsal fin, you will, or else probably you will have a straight one. Watch out for the rough-toothed dolphin. They can reach 350 pounds.

I told her that it was great. Don't change a word. They will tell you to change it, but you have to stand firm.

She said my story was pretty good, too. I asked her why. Then she admitted that she didn't like it very much, she was just trying to be nice. I said that's okay—she should know I actually did enjoy her dolphin story very much. She asked if I wanted her to try again with mine, and I said, no. She admitted that she didn't really read it. I was playing with my phone, she said.

Maybe I should put more animals in mine, she suggested. That's how she got hers started.

ENGLISH two

At the end, VanDuyn had everyone read the stories out loud, which was really painful. When it got to me I said I hadn't done it. Grace got a weird look on her face, but she kept quiet. She read hers, and she was honestly really proud in the way that she did it. I thought it was pretty beautiful that she could be so proud of such a terrible story. I am such a coward I could never have read my story to the class like that, no matter how good it was. So, Grace is a little ways ahead of me on the path of life, I honestly think.

After class, VanDuyn motioned me over to his desk. He said he was willing to give me some leeway because of my *situation,* but he would love to see what I wrote if I was prepared to show him. It's almost the worst thing when people are actually kind. It would be easier if they could all be creeps all the time.

Anyway, you are probably interested in hearing about my story, even if Grace didn't like it.

My story was called "MAY I SWEEP YOUR FRONT STEP." It was about a woman who lives in a house. One day a beggar comes and asks her if he can sweep her front doorstep. So, she lets him. The story doesn't start there, though. It starts in the future, at this refugee camp. There has been a disaster, and no one has a nice home anymore, but even in the refugee camp there is stratification, so some people have tents and others don't. Outside one of the tents, there is this guy sleeping, and he occasionally gets up and mimes sweeping the ground in front of the tent. Every now and then he lies down and sleeps some more, then gets up and repeats it. Someone asks the woman in the tent why he is doing this and she says, many years ago, she lived in a wealthy house in a big city and a man came to her house, a beggar, and he wanted to sweep her front step. She could tell that he was a suitor in disguise, and wanted to marry her. But, she let him sweep the front step, and she was kind of tricky, so whatever stratagems he would use to try to get more out of her, she would always reply with something more clever and he would have to keep sweeping.

Eventually, they grew old, and the disaster came, and she ended up in the camp with her tent, and the beggar shows up again, and he doesn't even have a broom, but still he sweeps the ground in front of the tent, this time with no broom. He doesn't even have a name anymore, she says, he has utterly become the costume he was wearing.

So, that was the story, but it was much better in reality, because it is all matter-of-fact. The woman doesn't see anything strange about any of it. Also, there is this thing about what the service actually is—what it is that the beggar is providing, and what it is he is taking. It is pretty hard to say who is winning.

PREDICTION

On this visit, I will go from my aunt's hospital to visit the Home, so the route will be different. There is actually a rail line that I can take, which is pretty exciting, since I have never taken it before. So, I will sneak on if I can without paying, or alternately, I will pay. I can't make a prediction about that until I know more. When I get to the Winston stop on the rail line, I will walk to the Home, this time from the other direction, and go up the drive, get my pass from the counter, go to my mom's room. She won't be there. But, she won't be at the fish pond either, because I think it will rain. She will probably then be under one of the gazebos. The place has at least ten gazebos. It seems like doctors think that gazebos are good for curing mental illness, because every asylum I have ever seen in reality (one) or in a film (five or six?) has gazebos everywhere. I guess some of the ones in films just look like prisons, so those don't have any gazebos, but I think it is mostly true.

Why that would be so—is hard to fathom. In my opinion, a gazebo should exacerbate mental illness, as it is a pretty unreasonable structure. It is poorly made, it doesn't provide any real shelter, and it is impossible to do any meaningful tasks inside of it. If a person is struggling to figure out the most basic rationales about life—is that the kind of place you want to stick them? It is pretty hard to understand.

Anyway, I will sit in the gazebo and witness my mother's gazebo behavior. I think that behavior will be a lot like the fish pond behavior. At some point the orderly will show up and we will pretend like nothing happened, but maybe he will give some overture to see what else he can get.

Then, I will head out and take the bus to the bus to the bowling alley and I will cry my face off telling Helen about my aunt, and she will give me a drink and I will wake up either at my aunt's house, or at Helen's. It doesn't really matter which.

WHAT HAPPENED

I saw my aunt, and she said she could go home definitely
the next day, or at least within the week. That was a real
comfort to me. The doctor was there and he gave me a
list of things that she shouldn't do. I said she doesn't do
anything anyway. He said she should eat these things,
and go to this physical therapy, et cetera. I pointed out
that it would be expensive to do that. Probably what
would happen is she would do what she has always done,
which is sit in her chair, tend her garden (which is not
really tending anything), and eat oatmeal and eggs and
shitty bread, and every now and then something fancy like
a bologna sandwich or something equally vile for dinner.
He looked at me over his glasses for a while and said it is
impossible to say how long she will hold out, and gave me
a bunch of numbers about the decrepitude of her organs,
which apparently had all already failed. I asked him if
he had bothered to have children. He said yes, he had
children. I said why if this is the result. He said I beg your
pardon. I said if it leads to this, where you're a skin bag
full of putrescent failing organs, and time passes quickly,
it passes so quickly, and he knew that, then why have
kids. He didn't like that, and his tone changed. He told me
some more bad things about my aunt's condition, signed
something with a real flourish, and went off.

WHAT HAPPENED

Well, then I went to the train, but my information I guess
was bad, because it only runs during rush hour. It was
raining and I would have gotten soaked, but I had my
raincoat on, so it was okay, but my bag was getting wet
and my shoes were soaked and I was pretty discouraged.

Then a taxi stopped and offered to take me for free since
the driver was going home and lived in that direction. He
was a young guy who had come there from Mozambique.
He said he drove two shifts per day and slept in between.
He showed me a picture of his wife, who is studying to
be a dentist. She had monster buckteeth, which I guess
if they are in good condition could be an advantage for a
dentist, like an advertisement of some sort. He confessed
that she was much smarter than he was, and so he would
support her for now, but in the end, it was he who would be
supported. I said that didn't sound dumb. It sounded like a
good deal for him. It is hard to stay awake, he said.

When we pulled into the drive and he let me out, he
asked why was I going to visit a mental hospital, and then
immediately he apologized and took back the question.
No, no, it's okay, I said, I sell medical equipment. I'm a rep
for a company. Sure you are, he agreed, and I got out.

There was a new guy at the desk, and so I had to run
through the whole rigmarole from the beginning.
Eventually, I got the pass, and headed down to my mom's
room. I was wrong about the gazebo. She was in her room.

I was dreading that, because it had happened once before that I tried to visit her in her room and she freaked out because she doesn't want anyone in there.

I think that's the reason why she is usually at the fish pond. If she is in her room she won't tolerate anyone she doesn't recognize, so the hospital personnel mostly just stick her there to sleep. The rest of the time, I guess, it is fish pond, gazebo, cafeteria, bathroom, whatever. I don't know all the rooms at the Home or I would list them for you.

I went to go into her bedroom area and she lost it. She was shouting for help, and I started crying. Then the nurse came, and it is lucky that my mom always behaves this way, because the nurse didn't blame me. Give me a minute she said, we'll take her to the bingo palace. I sort of curled up in the hall and waited, which was made even worse by the fact that my legs and feet and bag were wet. I was a real mess.

For some reason, my mom let this nurse woman calm her down and get her in the wheelchair, and then the three of us trundled along down to the bingo palace, which is a bizarre place. There are beans all over the tables, which I guess get used on the bingo cards. There are stacks and stacks of bingo cards. There is a stage with a podium. It is a pretty big production. The nurse had to turn on all the lights or none, so the whole huge room was lit, and she asked where we wanted to sit. I said, we might as well sit up there, so we sat on the stage where the bingo-caller sits.

Do you mind staying, I asked.

No, I don't mind.

I think my mom has been getting fatter since being in the loony bin. She has always been as thin as a stick, but now she is pretty heavy. When I look at her, it makes me wonder if there is anything left there that comprehends me. These are not the hands that touched me, this is not the mouth that kissed me, and so on.

I cried a little more, and the nurse squeezed my hand.

People here, she said, think it is wonderful the way you are with her. Don't think it doesn't matter what you do.

I hate being pitied. I just hate it. That's why I vowed to never mention anything about my parents to anyone, even if my aunt thinks it's the wrong way to handle it. She isn't always right.

Anyway, this woman is squeezing my hand and smiling like I'm a little saint, which you know is garbage.

Well, I got out of there pretty quick after that. I was dead right about Helen. She gave me as many drinks as I wanted, so I woke up with a blinding headache on her couch. Her cat was sleeping on me, and the morning sun was streaming through the window.

JAN

After school, Lana stopped me. She asked if I wanted to go roller skating, which isn't something I would have done anyway. I told her I was going to go meet some guys to talk about setting fires. Most people would be astonished by a statement like that, but Lana was just like, oh, cool, well, call me when you're done, maybe we'll still be out.

Also, she gave me back the story that I wrote, and she told me I was a good writer, but I could tell she didn't care about it. Good writer, like, one of those actual writers that nobody reads, one of the ones who leaves the good parts out. That's okay. I mean, I don't want to be the kind of person who writes just for fancy people or anything, so maybe it's a comeuppance. It's true, too: if she had really liked my high school writing, something would probably have been off. I mean in her head. I am realistic about things, don't you think?

I went down to Simonen again, and as it turned out, I was late because I took the bus too far. When I got there, Jan was there, but Stephan wasn't. He was leaning against a wall, smoking, and wearing a pretty roughed-up bomber jacket. He looked a little like an old cigarette ad in black and white.

Where's Stephan.

I told him to go home, Jan said. He's just a little boy.

That's weird, I said. Why would you do that.

LATE

Next day, I wasn't feeling very well, so I got to school a little
late, and Beekman caught me sneaking around in the hall.
I figured I was going to get hammered with a detention,
but no.

He says, you weren't in class this morning. I said, in a funny
voice I sometimes use on my aunt:

Darling, you must forgive me for getting home at dawn.
The boys and I were out whoring, and you know how that
can be.

He did that adult thing where he pretended to laugh but
didn't really laugh. I hate that thing. It's as if they want
you to know that they tried to laugh, but didn't laugh, at
your joke. But they tried to—they want credit for that. My
opinion about this is: if you didn't laugh at my joke, you
don't get credit. It's as simple as that. If you didn't laugh,
you didn't find it funny. Why would I give you credit, which
is essentially deciding we have a similar outlook, at least
on this matter, if you are demonstrating if anything the
opposite? In this case it wasn't even a joke, not really.
I guess I was showing off a bit.

He said, I was going to tell you—I found a program that
might be good. Have a look. He pulls this envelope out of
his pocket and hands it to me. There is a test to get in, and
anyone can take it. One of the places you can test is near
here—and it's next week. I or one of the other teachers
would drive you, if you needed it.

Thanks.

He went away and I went into the bathroom to look at it. One of the stalls is broken, so no one ever uses it. I went in there and opened the envelope.

HAUSMANN

The place, Hausmann, was a one- or two-year school for kids who are fourteen to sixteen and (I guess) who hate school. That's what I got out of the materials. You go to this place, which is somewhere really nice, like Maine or Vermont, I don't know, and you stay there for one year or two depending, and at the end of it, if you feel like it, you go on to college, which would be a year or two early, and basically every last one of the shits gets into a great school (97 percent, which I guess means one or two kids probably offed themselves and ruined the numbers—kids like that must off themselves at a furious rate, that would be my expectation).

Well, I don't care about college, but this is free, they say, if you pass the test, and the courses looked way better than Whistler. Then I thought about my aunt and I felt bad. I think she's pretty used to having me around.

Beekman had written on the envelope, *Lucia, it's very prestigious, and I think you have a shot.*

If by prestigious, he means for delinquents, then yes, I have a shot.

One of the pictures showed some girls rock climbing. Another showed a guy skeet shooting while someone else next to him, I kid you not, writes equations on a pad of paper. You know, the old tandem shotgun shooting + math lesson—that's how it's always done . . .

The kids in the pictures weren't scrawny with beady eyes like I expected. They looked on the whole pretty normal. I thought of how neat it would be if a place somehow made promotional materials that had a little camera in them, and that they could then take your picture without you knowing. Then when you looked at the pictures, it would be you rock climbing, you skeet shooting, you taking dumb notes on a pad of paper next to yourself holding a shotgun. On second thought that is a terrible idea. Forget I mentioned it.

I found Beekman after lunch and asked him if he knew what the test was like. He said,

Yes, it is in three parts. There's an IQ test, an essay question, and an oral part—a video you record in response to a question, sort of like an interview.

That sounds horrible.

Well, you don't have to do it.

Thanks anyway.

He looked a little hurt.

Maybe I will, I said. I'll think about it.

how to set a fire and why

This is what happened. Jan and I jumped the fence and went in. He did in about three seconds, but I had to scramble over. I mean, he is about a foot taller than me after all. When I got to the other side, he announced:

He was going to set one of the project buildings on fire.

He actually said, it's my intention to burn one of those project buildings to the ground. I thought that was a little grandiose, so I spat in the gravel. Was that me trying to do some cool guy stuff? Maybe it was. Thinking back it sounds kind of lame. I'm glad Lana and Ree weren't there to see it.

As we walked, he told me a lot of stuff. Maybe he noticed I was nervous, because he told me that he was not going to do anything to me in the building, that I didn't have to worry about that. He said I should stay outside and keep watch.

Keep watch? There's no one here.

What is your name again? Lucia?

(I know he knows my name.)

Lucia, listen up: the first rule of setting fires is that someone should keep watch. Human beings are notorious for being where they aren't supposed to be. Do you want your whole life to be ruined because some asshole is walking his dog and remembers your face? Such a pretty face, too.

He ran his hand through my hair and it creeped me out, but I didn't say anything. I let him do it, I guess. We kept walking.

When we got inside, he took his coat off and put on a bright-colored jacket. I asked him why he would wear a bright jacket.

Afterwards, I get rid of it, he said. Obviously.

I still wasn't sure that was the best idea—but I kept my mouth shut.

The field was uneven, so it wasn't easy to cross it in the dark, and when I turned on my flashlight, Jan smacked me in the arm.

Off.

I shut it off.

He got a little ahead of me, and I ran to catch up.

Stephan just went home, huh.

He does what he's told to do. The things Sco and me used to do to him when he was little, ha. Once we made him crawl through a thornbush. We told him it would be cool and he did it.

His brother's in the army, yeah?

I don't know. I don't care about that guy. He can do what the fuck he wants.

When we got to the building, Jan took a bottle of something out of his backpack. Gasoline?

It's like gasoline, he said. Something like that. Wait here.

There was a stoop next to where the street had been, so, I went up to the fourth step and sat down. I couldn't hear anything from inside. The building had just swallowed him up. Any number of people could disappear into it.

I smoked. I waited. I smoked another cigarette, another cigarette. I would have smoked another, but it was my last. It must have been half an hour later when I heard someone running and Jan shot out of the building.

Book it, he said, and grabbed my arm. We set out sprinting across the field. I tripped two or three times, but got right up and kept going. Somehow Jan stayed on his feet the whole way. When we got to the other side, there was a huge pile of tires.

This should do, he said, and got behind it.

I don't know what the fuck is in there, so I don't want to be near it if a gas line blows.

Nothing

and

nothing

and

nothing.

I was looking into the black and breathing hard. I couldn't even really see the building, just an outline of all the buildings where the darkness got lighter in the distance. Then, I thought I heard something, and WHOOSH!

That whole half of the world turned red. It was like a huge flame tongue erupted out of all the windows at the same time. It flashed away and I couldn't see anything at all, and then a half second later, there was more, this time it was smaller flames that came, but they stayed, all along one line—about halfway up the building I'd guess.

Jan put his arm around me, but not in a bad way—it was a celebration, like you'd do with anyone. I didn't mind.

Do you think there was anybody in there? Some vagrant sleeping?

I checked, said Jan. That's what took so long. I wouldn't do it for most places, but I don't want to kill some homeless guy or leave him covered in burns. Come on, let's get out of here.

We climbed down to the street, and after we'd gone a block or two Jan tossed his jacket in a sewer drain.

He looked at me and didn't say anything, and then he did.

Now you're in the club. You held it together. Most people can't do that. I figured you'd be gone when I came out.

The school Arson Club?

Ha, no. There isn't one. That's just nonsense.

He waited for my bus to come (once per hour) and told me some more stuff, which I was eager to hear. He was suddenly really jovial. He kept touching my arm and relating little bits of nonsense. I think he was proud of himself for setting the fire. Truth is—I felt really good, too. The feeling of setting a fire is enormous, so even helping out like I did—I was in the clouds.

About the club, he said the way it works is—if you want to talk about the club, the actual club for the area gets members from the schools. Only two other people in my school were in so far. The rest were just wannabes like Stephan.

But now you, you can come to the real meetings, he said. And one more thing maybe you've guessed already—you can't tell anyone you're in. It's the opposite. Now you tell them you're done with setting fires, you're over it. Got it? Give them the high hat. Since I'm a recruiter, I stay in the open. But now you're behind doors. Don't breathe a fucking word.

I got home, took my clothes off, got in bed and lay there in the dark. It's pretty lonely being alone in a house—in one where you usually have company. I suppose that's a moronic sentence. It's lonely being alone, but I felt that way. I'm often alone and I don't feel lonely, but going to sleep in that converted garage without my aunt there, it was terrible. I tried to pretend she was slumped in the chair. I propped up the blue blanket so it looked like it was covering something and it actually made me feel better. Then, I lay down again and thought about the fire.

I thought about that immaculate blankness. It had been too much for my eyes—my eyes had just given up.

I know it was just an abandoned building, but I felt like something had happened, a real thing for once. My aunt's stroke had felt pretty real too. I guess real things happen all at once, and then you go back to the false parade of garbage that characterizes modern life.

Well, I don't want to go back there.

Thinking something like that, I fell asleep.

AUNT

While I was waiting in the hospital for the elevator, I noticed a flyer for a psych experiment. It said it would pay one hundred dollars and it lasts fifteen minutes. Women eighteen to thirty-five with perfect eyesight.

I thought—why not?

So, after I saw my aunt, I headed down there.

My aunt, in case you are wondering, was still alive. I wasn't going to have to go visit her in the hospital anymore, because they were to return her to the house soon. That meant I had a lot to do—cleaning up the place, getting some groceries (shoplifting some groceries), et cetera, but there was time.

She seemed in good spirits. She should have been, since I gave her the book I made—it's not like it's nothing!

She wanted to read it while I was there, but I refused. What an awful idea. There is no way to save face if someone reads your shit while you stand there. Much better to get out immediately. If they like it, actually, that fact can come up later or not. I would have stayed longer but I felt like I did my due diligence with the gift. Also, the hospital room smelled awful.

The study was being conducted in the psych department of the university hospital. That was in a different building,

but the buildings are all connected, so I wandered around
for forty minutes going this way on one bridge and that
way on another until I found it. I pictured it like some old
French movie where the shot is from far away and sped up,
and you can see me through the glass bridges and windows
going back and forth. Maybe I would be riding a bicycle
some of the time for no reason, and being chased by a
gorilla.

CORRINGER LAB

A girl in her mid-thirties wearing a lab coat answered the door when I knocked.

She was heavyset and had a voice like a man, which was sort of endearing. I don't mean just deep—I mean, she sounded exactly like a man. It was neat.

Come in, she said. You are eighteen, right?

I showed her the license I stole from the girl at my school. She is a senior, and turned eighteen in January, which put me in the clear.

Here's a fact: no one really looks at IDs. I don't know why they bother putting pictures on them. What they do is— they look at you and decide if they like you or not.

The researcher, Mary, told me to sit down. The room had a table and two chairs. There were some computers and a couch. There was a big whiteboard with some crap written on it—scientist handwriting, practically unreadable.

I leaned on the edge of the couch and waited.

You can sit down, she said.

No thanks, I said.

Your eyesight is perfect, yes?

Yes.

She gave me some forms to fill out. I did so, but had to look at the ID to remember the girl's fucking last name. How stupid is that. I have a decent memory, but this was a Polish name with twelve consonants in a row. I bet you couldn't remember it either.

Luckily the researcher wasn't watching. When I gave her the forms she showed me into the next room.

Stand there, she said.

There was a circle drawn on the floor. I went and stood in it.

Images will show up on the far side of the room. Images of people in profile. You are being recorded. I want you to state, whenever an image appears, what you think the age and sex of the person being shown is. Tap your leg if you find them threatening.

For fifteen minutes, silhouettes flashed on the screen: thirties male unthreatening. Sixties male threatening. Infant female threatening. Et cetera.

Actually, I did try to do a good job. I like trying at things like that.

A loud beep sounded when the final image was done. The door behind me opened, and Mary came and gave me a hundred bucks cash in five-dollar bills. I love getting a

thick pile of bills. Even though I hate money. Of course I
do, I hate it. But I also like to have lots of it. Once, I had
three hundred dollars at the same time, when I pawned my
dad's watch. They gave me three hundred singles. I said to
the pawnshop guy, I'm not on my way to a strip club. He
thought that was funny, so we had a good laugh for about
three seconds. I mean, I was fourteen so he shouldn't have
laughed at all.

By the way, I wouldn't have sold it if I thought my dad cared
about the watch, but he told me once that he only wore it
because his grandfather had given it to him. That might be
a reason for him to wear it, but for me—not so much.

Mary opened the door for me to go, and I asked her if she
would tell me what the study was about.

I don't see why not. Don't go telling people if you think they
might come in, though. That would ruin the study.

Obviously it would ruin the study. I wouldn't do that.

Good. So, identifying the silhouettes is meaningless. The
actual experiment is: we change the temperature of the
room to see how it affects your threat level. That's it.

But how do you know which ones are threatening or not to
begin with?

We run the study without the temperature shift until we
have five hundred samples, average them, and then run it
again, this time changing the temperature.

Why just women?

We do it with men and women, both. We did men already, now women.

What do you think you'll find?

James, the PI, thinks men will be more threatened by heat, and women by cold.

What do you think?

He is usually wrong about things. But, we get interesting results, so that's enough.

I laughed at that. She didn't.

One more question. Sorry to take up your time.

Shoot.

Which of the silhouettes is supposed to be the most threatening one?

There's one, do you remember, an old woman carrying groceries? It's totally terrifying. Men especially fear it. Women are pretty afraid of the baby. They don't actually tap their leg, but they start to and then stop.

CORRINGER LAB

I was waiting at the bus stop when I realized that my zippo was gone. What a pain—I had to backtrack, first to my aunt's room, then to the study. When I got to the study, I could see Mary wasn't happy to see me. I had to bang on the door to get her to answer it.

When the door opened, I could see there were three girls in the room who looked like triplets. I was a bit shocked, and I think Mary was trying to figure out if it would fuck up the study to have triplets in it, what with them being essentially the same person. They were wearing the same tricolor tube top with some sorority name on it.

Which reminds me: I don't buy this thing about twins both getting to vote. To me, each group of DNA should get one vote. Also, twins shouldn't both be able to hold political office. Otherwise, things could get weird—not in the short run, but in the long run, watch out! I mean, imagine if someone had identical septuplets and then all seven of them were appointed to the Supreme Court. I guess there are nine justices, so let's say nonuplets then. You have nine identical twins, raised on some creepy farm and then carted out to be Supreme Court justices. What would that mean? It would mean essentially you have one person being the whole Supreme Court, for life! I ask you, would that be fair?

I'm just joking, I have a whole bunch of friends who are identical twins. They're really nice if you get to know them.

Mary reached in her pocket, handed me my shitty lighter, and shut the door.

TEST

My aunt thought it was a good idea for me to go with
Beekman and take the test. She is a straight shooter, you
know, so what she said was:

I don't think I will live out the year and then what will
you do.

To which I said, aunt, don't be a fool. And she said, who is
the fool. I will be a bunch of soil and you'll be living where?

So, I told Beekman I would go. On Saturday morning,
he came and picked me up. His wife actually packed me
a goddamned lunch with a pluot in it. She is a big fan of
yours, he said.

The test center was at the admissions department of a
local university, which I guess did this as some sort of
helping gesture for Hausmann. Apparently a lot of schools
countrywide have agreements like this. Hausmann was
started because there are a large number of talented
kids who go on to do nothing at all—they turn into
misanthropes and huddle in shitty rooms. The idea was—
reach these kids earlier, challenge them, some nonsense
like that. My feeling about that is—doing nothing doesn't
necessarily prove your incapacity. It could be quite the
opposite. For instance—I walk around and I am always
identifying places, under overpasses, beneath pine trees in
industrial parks, at the verge of people's yards, or where a
park building meets a factory and there is a dry spot, these

are examples: I see these places, and I think, I could just stay in a spot like that and be perfectly happy. If I did that, it would look to other people like I had failed, but it sounds wonderful to me.

Beekman brought me into the building and introduced me to the admissions officer. Then he wished me luck and left.

Is he coming back? the woman asked me.

I hope so, I said. It is a long fucking walk.

She gave me a look and showed me into a conference room. You can take the test in here, she said.

A different woman, a psychologist of some sort, came in. She introduced herself. Her name was Tracy. I was a little nervous.

Is that your real name, I asked.

Yes, of course.

I just thought, maybe the test had started already. I figured maybe your name isn't Tracy and I'm supposed to notice that. You look about thirty-four, thirty-five. That means you were born in a period when, uh, when Tracy was a pretty popular name. So, it is likely to be your real name. Although, it seems like maybe—since the likelihood of you having a likely name is unlikely, since there are all told more unlikely names than likely names, if you have a likely name, it seems like maybe you chose it to seem like it is your real name. Isn't that so? Is this part of the test?

My name is Tracy, she said. Let's get started.

Okay. So it's not part of the test? How do I know when the test starts?

It hasn't started yet. Calm down. Do you need a drink of water?

No.

The first part we're going to do is the IQ test. Have you taken some practice IQ tests to get ready?

I told her I had not. I said why would I take a practice IQ test. It wouldn't increase my IQ.

She said that it doesn't increase your IQ, no, just your demonstrable IQ as tested.

I said that means the test is bad. There should be no way to increase your result on a good IQ test. It should be tricky enough to avoid that.

She said it is not tricky enough to avoid that.

You will probably be smarter than your result, then, she said. That's too bad.

Which is a weird way of saying I'm going to mess it up.

When we got done with the IQ test, I got a break. They brought me an orange juice and a buttered roll and let me sit on a bench outside for twenty minutes. The university grounds are really beautiful. Universities always try that bullshit. They want you to think wonderful things are going on inside of them because the grounds are beautiful. In general, it is good to be suspicious of monetary displays. Large swaths of bright green well-watered grass—a thing like that is a huge lie.

They called me back in and gave me an exam booklet. There was a question written on the board. The question was:

Why Hitler?

On the first page of the exam booklet it said I could write as much or as little as I felt like. It said it in this way:

An answer of any length might be sufficient.

I thought about it for a little bit and didn't write anything. I figured the fewer cross-outs the better. Also—I figure, any part of it might be the test, so I should hoof it and get something down, since they might be watching through a camera and might disallow whatever I write after the first five minutes. That's how I would do the test, if I were them. My aunt would think of some even sneakier shit, I bet. Like, someone talks to you in the waiting room before the test, and that is the test.

I thought about that, and then thought about thinking about that, about her, and then I thought about her husband and how it was funny that in his letter he hadn't seemed that smart, but maybe he was smart in some other way. Or maybe he was nervous writing letters from a military barracks, so he did it in a strictly ordinary way. That could be why she kept the letter. It was some sort of bravura performance of writing a lame soldier-letter-home-to-his-sweetheart. I bet there are coded parts I didn't understand.

So, *why Hitler?*

There are a few questions I could answer. I figure the test wasn't so much about what I wrote, but about which question I could intuit.

Why Hitler? could be:

Why was "Hitler" the one who committed a nice fat genocide and captivated the world as a figure of evil, where "Hitler" is the particular archetype of a Hitler sort of person, of which there might be several. If you imagine there are many sorts of evil archetypes, the question could be—why this "Hitler" rather than a different Hitler. In other words, if the world were a bit more faintly greenish colored, and a butterfly flapped its wings into tatters in a zoological garden in Brussels, maybe the Hitler that we would have gotten would have been a different one. Maybe he would have loved peacocks or something, and used gypsy musicians for his military marching bands. He'd still have been bad—just a different sort of bad, right?

According to this logic, I would have to say, my answer is: pick any event, historically, that you want: the dauphin stubbing his toe, for instance, and it'll lead you right on to this particular "Hitler." Change any of those things, and you get peacock Hitler. We'll just class whichever of the other Hitlers gets chosen as peacock Hitler. You understand, we aren't specifying anything other than that he's the one who appears when the dauphin doesn't stub his toe.

But, there are other why Hitlers, and maybe a different one is more interesting. It could be why Hitler?, as in, why did this man, "Hitler," manage to become Hitler? As in, within the span of his life, how did an ordinary person transform into a monstrous sort of venal godhead and can the reason be found in his actual physical body, or was it just the events that surrounded him and swept him along? So, in my answer, I would be choosing from between those two, sort of a nature versus nurture thing.

A third option is, why Hitler?, as in, why are we asking you about Hitler? That's a tricky question. There are some obvious answers, like because the idea of Hitler freaks people out and makes them behave badly. It reduces people to intellectual weaklings often. So, the why there would be—because you are trying to reduce me to an intellectual weakling.

Another reason along those lines is: to get rid of a cultural advantage. Pretty much everyone has heard about Hitler and can say some clever Hitler stuff, so it doesn't test historical knowledge very much. I mean, maybe there's a Malaysian punk band called Hitler, and if somebody writes about that, they do fine.

But, I think the best question asked by the question, why Hitler? is: why do we as humans refuse to recognize that a life has fixed proportions and can't go beyond itself? Why do we allow people to be blown up into monstrous caricatures of celebrity that extend to such grotesque lengths that they efface our lives, the only lives that are real? In other words—the existence of Hitlers makes you putting your shoe on a bit trivial. But it isn't trivial at all, it's your shoe!

The answer to that question is more complicated. It is possibly a question that is deserving of an answer. But, I am definitely not prepared to answer it.

So, I just wrote down this whole angle of thought with all the various questions they might be asking and then a part at the end where I apologize for giving up, but mention that: I think it is connected with man's fruitless search for meaning, sorry if that's a cop-out.

There was a little bell and when I rang it, Tracy came in, gave me a banana, and told me I could take another twenty-minute break. I walked down to a lake that was next to the chemistry building and watched some turtles hang out on a log. Being a turtle is essentially a royal flush in the game of life. Things can't eat you. You hang out in the sun. I don't know what they eat, but they don't look very hungry. If they were they would have evolved the ability to move faster so they could stop being so hungry.

The final part of the test was also in that room. When I got back, Tracy had set up a camera on a tripod. It was facing a box outlined on the wall.

The camera can see the whole box, she said. Once I start it, anything in the box is recorded.

And sound anywhere in the room, I said.

That's right, sound too.

Is the only microphone in the camera?

That's the microphone.

Can I see what the image looks like?

She thought about that for a second.

No, you can't. All right, I'm going to read you a script. Then, I'll leave. The camera starts recording a few seconds after I leave. I think it is a five-second delay. Also, if you want to use the chalkboard, there is chalk there below.

Great.

Here we go.

She read from the sheet:

Tell us a joke.

She left the room.

I brought a chair over and sat with my back to the camera. I didn't like having it look at me.

TELL US A JOKE

Beekman said that a high-enough score on any one of the three tests could get you in, but good results on all three would not. I thought that was a mean thing to say, and not very helpful, though I'm sure he meant well. Anyway, I don't even know why I cared about passing the test. If I'm competitive, it's usually about things that don't matter to other people.

TELL US A JOKE

When I get in a tough spot, as you might have noticed, I like to think about what my aunt or my dad would do. I used to think about my mom like that, too. Don't think she isn't a fascinating character in her own right—just as great as my dad or aunt. But, thinking about her, well, it just doesn't get me anywhere anymore. Even now, I wish I hadn't brought it up.

TELL US A JOKE

I hate telling jokes on command. It has to be one of the worst situations a person can be in. That's why you have to respect the jesters of medieval times. They were always ready to be funny, but in exchange they forfeited all dignity—and in return, they got a special kind of permanent dignity that wasn't destroyed by scrounging around with the dogs to get a scrap now and then. Or that's how it's been told to me. Maybe there weren't even jesters. Have they ever found any jester bones? If they have, I certainly haven't seen them. That would be something—to see a full set of jester bones in a museum, strung up like an ankylosaurus.

The funniest things are usually the most revealing.
I thought about Lana and I thought—she is really good at
telling stories. I'll just tell one of the stories that she told me
the first time we hung out.

I turned my chair around.

TELL US A JOKE

Okay, so this is a true story. There is a golden eagle that was being observed by scientists, and it found a spot on top of this cathedral where it could nest. It liked that spot pretty well. I think there ended up being two of them— which means it somehow convinced another one the spot was good, but that isn't part of the story. The story goes like this: the eagle looks around for food in the town, but it is having trouble finding food, so it starts hunting people's dogs. First it kills a Chihuahua. Then, it kills a Yorkie. It catches a guy with his Belgian Malinois on his back stairs and whips the Malinois off so it falls to its death, then it drags it god knows where to have a nice meal.

Okay, so this is funny to begin with. I mean, if you like this sort of thing. But, what's funnier is this: one day it kills this beagle, and the beagle is wearing a kind of stupid knit party hat. While it is eating the beagle, I guess the beagle turned out to be a good meal and the golden eagle lost its cool, the knit party hat, which was bright purple and green, gets transferred onto the eagle's head. It gets stuck there, somehow it is thoroughly stuck to the eagle's head. What does this mean? And this is the joke: for the next two months, people were running around in this town pulling on their dogs' leashes and looking to the sky for an eagle wearing a party hat. And sometimes the eagle comes. There's even a video of it—the eagle is doing a cool eagle dive, and the party hat is flapping ominously in the wind.

BEEKMAN

Beekman asked me how it went, and I said: they don't
let you down these Hausmann people. That is a real test.
I mean—certainly you can chop up a group of people with
that test. You can slice them up real thin.

He asked me if I got sliced up thin.

I said, it was more like in a dream where I was both being
sliced and the one slicing.

Beekman told me about a samurai sword exhibit he took
his son to once and how the blades are all very beautiful
but you know that each and every one got tested on a
peasant's back.

GARDEN

When I got home, my aunt was sitting in the garden. She was drawing a diagram on a piece of paper. I sat next to her.

What is that?

It is for you, she said. I am preparing a plan for you to make a garden like this if you want to, sometime in the future.

Her rules were: plant some things almost randomly. Let weeds grow. If you like the weeds, then weed the plants out.

She had a diagram with all the beds that looked like this:

BED (weeds)	BED (garlic)	BED (weeds)
BED (carrots)	BED (weeds)	BED (weeds)
BED (dirt)	BED (dill/weeds)	BED (

She wasn't finished yet.

How did the test go?

I kind of kicked at the ground a bit and didn't say anything. My right sneaker had a huge hole and you could see my big toe sometimes.

We need to get you some new shoes, she observed. I think there is a box with a few pairs in it at the church.

I said, Beekman was pretty nice, telling me about the test.

She said she had talked to Beekman on the phone and he seemed, yes, like a nice man. I asked her why she had talked to him on the phone.

She said he had called. She answered the phone. Then she was talking to him on the phone. That was the order of events.

I said, but why did he call?

She said, he needed permission if he was going to give me a ride somewhere. Otherwise he could be accused of all sorts of bad business.

That's the world we live in, she said.

We sat there for a while. I noticed that her hands were shaky as hell. They are just trembling and trembling. It made my stomach feel funny.

Lucia, dear, did you ever think that maybe I died already— when the ambulance came for me, and that you have just been imagining all this ever since because your mind can't cope with the reality of the situation? Right now, you are just sitting here by yourself in the garden, for instance, and . . .

Stop it! Stop it! Stop it!

My aunt likes to put it on me sometimes. She calls that sort of thing an *improvement lesson.*

I'm just bringing you up to snuff, she says.

THE PAMPHLET!

And now I will put in my pamphlet (after this).

It's my opinion that you will find it to be quite interesting.
Of course, you may hate it, and that would be completely
understandable. I tried to make the language more
formal—since I was imagining as I went that I don't know
who will read it. Sometimes you put a thing out into the
wind, and the wind carries it—to where?

There are a few copies of this. My aunt has one. Lana has
one. I stuck one in the library at school, somewhere it won't
be discovered for years.

You have seen the cover—I stuck that in earlier. So, I'll just
jump to the first page.

INTRODUCTION

I am writing this for you who are so much like me. I have discovered some fine and plain things, and it is those things that I am giving to you in this pamphlet, the little monograph called:

HOW TO SET A FIRE
AND WHY

Some people look at a thing and think, *oh, this is not a thing that is for me.* Well, you needn't do that here, because this is for you—just for you.

The world is ludicrous. It is famished. It is greedy and adulterous. It is a wild place we inhabit, surely you agree? Well, then we shall have to try to make some sense of it. That is part of the reason why I have made this pamphlet. It is a kind of grip that you can have on the world. You can hold on to this, and find your way forward. That's what I'm promising you.

LUCIA STANTON

LIST OF FIRST THINGS

I want you to go out and buy yourself a lighter or a good box of matches. If they are matches, it is nice for them to be strike-anywhere matches. Those are the best kind. The lighter does not have to be a very nice one. In fact, it should be fairly nondescript, if possible. You will keep it in your pocket as a sort of token. Stick your hand in there now and then as you go around and remember: all the buildings that exist, all the grand structures of wealth and power, they remain standing because you permit them to remain. With this little lick of flame in your pocket, with this little gift of Prometheus, you can reduce everyone to a sort of grim equality. All those who ride on the high horse may be made to walk. Therefore, when you are at the bank and the bank manager speaks roughly to you, when you are denied entrance to a restaurant or other place of business, when you are made to work longer than you should need to, when you are driven out of your own little dwelling and made to live in the street, reach into your pocket, caress your own little vehicle of flame, and feel the comfort there.

We shall set fires—and when we set them, we shall know why.

POOR OR RICH

It is not important to me whether you are at this moment poor or rich. If you have the requisite humanity in your heart, the substance of empathy, then you will leave these classes, the poor, the rich, and join a new class: that is, the class of those who subsist gladly and meagerly. This is the class of least things. We want merely to have that which is necessary and least, and it is our joy to share what is necessary and least with others. Do you see this? We want to have nothing that we cannot share. We want to have an empathy that says: *it would hurt me to have a thing that others cannot have.*

What do we hate? We hate when we see people prevented from having what is necessary and least. Others may talk of owning horses and riding in elegant machines on broad roads built just for them. We deplore such things. What's more, we have an intention, and our intention is this:

WE
WILL
BURN
THEM
OUT

Whether I do it today, whether you do it tomorrow, whether someone you speak to, a person who has never known and never will know me, does it in the days to come, it matters not the least. Still it will happen that the lower shall rise to burn away what is above.

There is a simple thing to remember—what is the measure?

What is the measure of need? It is this: a person naturally enforces the space of her need. If a man is away from his house and you want to sleep there, then sleep there. It is a house, it is for sleeping. If he returns and you are there, and there is no space for two to sleep, then you sleep side by side in what little space there is, and you set to building another small shelter, so that you both may have a roof. It is a thing you do together.

That it seems impossible for such kindness to exist is only for one reason:

Wealth squeezes us, the wealthy squeeze us and squeeze us, until we cannot even help one another as we would naturally do, as it is already in our hearts to do.

Never let yourself be squeezed in this way. My dear friend, my heart, resist it!

ALL THINGS THAT ARE BUILT MAY BURN

Everything that is built will burn, or if it will not burn it may be wrecked. If it cannot be wrecked, it may be poisoned so that it stands as an example. This is not just a book about fire, although fire is our joy. It is a book about how we may share what is least, and the first step toward this sharing is that we must abolish the having of the most. We must convince the wealthy that they cannot have more than they need. When they are convinced of that, they will be like us. They will be acceptable to us. We will greet them with open arms.

JOY OF FIRES

Oh, the joy of fires! If you have ever lit a candle, then you know the exquisite pleasure that fire brings. It is the visible aspect of man's wit and cunning. It is the smallest and most complete mastery. To set a thing ablaze and thereby without effort change what it is—and cause light, and cause heat, and cause smoke.

I walk into the woods a short way to a clearing, a place I went to often as a small child. There I pile some branches. I make a sort of structure out of kindling—a very tiny building, and I burn that building, this little building I have built and in its burning, it lights the logs above. You see, even setting a campfire is a sort of arson.

But, ARSON, what is it? Certainly it must be one of the most beautiful words. Arson, arson—how it rolls from the tongue! I should be so lucky as to be an arsonist. What a sentence it would be to say: *an arsonist lives safely in a cellar.*

We deceive ourselves into thinking life is long, but fire reminds us—it is a flickering. Life is a flickering—and then it is gone. So, we must make the most of it.

Fire is red. It is yellow. It is blue. It is black as ash, brown as seared lines on timbers. Fire is the pink of flesh, and the gray of smoke that trails. Fire is the all-color that dwells before color, that which comes when one feels a fire will be set—but upon what, but how?

When there is a fire, people run from their houses—not to safety, but to where the fire is, to the house that is burning, in order to see it. They are not coming to help. They simply want to see a conflagration.

I played a game once with a friend when I was nine. We had

two capes—stupid capes that were made for us in the days before a Halloween. What if, she said to me, we light them on fire and run, and the first one to take off her cape loses.

Such aspirations are the joy of fire—we feel in fire we shall be tested. And indeed, fire has always been the final test. How shall we know a witch? With water—or with fire. And then to settle the question, we shall burn her—that is what they used to say.

WHERE YOU LIVE

You sit with this pamphlet in a house or on a bench, and around you there stretches a neighborhood, and beyond that other neighborhoods. Or perhaps you are in the country—and there are just fields, and beyond those fields, before you may reach a town. Still, with a little effort you may, I'm sure, come to a place where a building is: a tall building, a building that you hate. One you would see burned if you could. I tell you, my dear friend, set your heart upon that building. You shall burn it. Each day when you pass, picture the building in flames. Each night before sleep call up its face and see

how it will be when you throw your little match in just the right spot. Imagine the delight, the slow-rising joy that will stretch through your toes, legs, limbs, the cavity of your chest and up across the muscles of your face as you behold that tall building shivering in fiery tatters. It will be a blow that you have struck on behalf of all who are human— and who wish to be human. Only those who wish to have a place above us—only those will lament what you have done.

PRACTICAL MATTERS

The simplest way to set fire to a building is to use what are called accelerants. Gasoline, for instance, helps to cause a fire, as everyone knows. Likewise, the gas that comes out of stoves, or that is used for heating. If set fire to, it shall yield marvelous results. There are many types of accelerants—the difficulty with them is this: often it can be discovered in the ruins of the building that a fire was set and how, by the presence of those accelerants. You see, they do not burn themselves away completely. It was once the case that the police laboratories were ill managed and overburdened, but their methods have advanced, and it is a sure thing—if a decent investigator comes to the site of your arson, the fact of it will be discovered. Of course, this is a far cry from saying that you will be discovered. In fact, even if you would be discovered, proving arson is extremely difficult in court, so there is every chance that you would get away (especially if you have no reason to have burned the building). And too—who is to say that you personally will ever be discovered? It is a sharp arson investigator who can find a person who has burned a building without hope of remuneration, and without desire for revenge. The very fact that you don't want anything is what will protect you.

K

A good way to set a fire and have it appear ordinary and natural is to use a cigarette to set off the gas from a stove or oven. If you let the gas build for long enough, it will be sufficient. If you don't mind having it known that it was arson, you can do this: break into a house, make sure all the doors and windows are shut tight. Go into the kitchen, shut the doors to the kitchen. Close all vents—if they won't close, stuff them with cloth. Turn on all the burners, but do not let them spark. Simply let the gas flow out. Let it fill that room for a while. Go into the next room. Light a candle so that when the candle has burned down, it will pass through a cloth taper that you have drenched in gasoline. That taper should stretch all the way under the door of the room to the kitchen. Thus you may with ordinary materials create a fine explosion and burn a house down! What's nice about that particular arrangement is that you needn't be in the house at all when it happens.

PROTECTING THE FIRE

It would be a sad thing if the fire that you made was put out almost immediately by firemen, wouldn't it? That is why a good arsonist learns to protect his/her fire. How can a fire be protected? There are several ways.

1. If you are in league with others (as in an Arson Club or other such syndicate or organization), then declare the appointed time that your fire shall start. Let each

of these individuals go to places near the sector where your fire will be and pull fire alarms in various critical buildings (hospitals, city halls, et cetera). Let them report fires via telephone. Let them make diffuse the efforts of the fire department so that your true fire is just one of many apparent fires. Your fire will then have a chance to burn and grow.

2. Cause mayhem on the roads leading to your fire. You can do this with a gesture as simple as breaking the traffic lights at a few intersections, spreading caltrops (multi-pointed metal objects to be littered on the ground to pierce tires). Perhaps you have seen that the police have a specific tool which they put across roads to destroy tires in automotive pursuits. Such a thing can be easily created in a workshop. It is a long metal beam with teeth and can be made to be flat and yanked up at the appropriate time.

3. I have heard it said that it is possible to actually enter a fire department and sabotage the trucks. I am sure this is so—

but it seems so prohibitively difficult that I would not advise it unless you are a real expert at conducting operations. In the case of a truly giant fire of colossal importance—if you were, for instance, burning down a courthouse or a corporate headquarters—it might be worthwhile to sacrifice a group of men or women, perhaps nine or ten, who would act as snipers, positioned in buildings across from each of the closest fire departments. These people (who would expect to be caught, be tortured, die, et cetera) could prevent the fire trucks from leaving the station, and ensure that your fire was protected for as long as possible.

ON ACCOMPLICES

While it is generally better to not have accomplices, it is true also that certain enterprises are of a scale that they cannot be performed alone. If you are to have accomplices, it should be the case that the thing you hope to accomplish is worthy of the danger that you will be betrayed, whether by foolishness or rancor.

If your syndicate or Arson Club stretches its wings far enough—it may be possible for you to execute a clever maneuver. We shall call it: reciprocal action. In this case, you are in danger of being accused of committing arson simply by living in the vicinity of the fire. That much is apparent, no? The pool of possible suspects is drawn from those who might have done it—from those who are alive, for instance (they do not search the graveyards). So, if you can bring a person from a far place, who passes through undetected and commits the act of arson that you would have committed, then it will be very difficult for the arm of the law to find this person, absent travel records, and a great effort can be made to avoid the creation of such records.

Then you, or someone from your association, would travel to the place of residence of your benefactor, and would commit an arson in that vicinity and return with no one the wiser. Even better, Arson Clubs would simply pass this sort of favor on to one another without hope of recompense.

ON ANGER

When committing an act of arson, you should be completely calm. You must never let yourself be blinded by anger. Even if you are setting fire to the bank that has caused you and others great injury, and a righteous anger fills you as you pour gasoline into the vault— even then you should not permit yourself this. You do not do these things for revenge. You do not do them out of anger. You do them to find a way into the hearts of all living humans, to show them that we can all live with what is least, with what is meager. We can share these things together and be glad. Have that feeling fill you as you set your fires.

TWO LIVES

It is a sad fact that we live in a surveillance state. You will perhaps be seen entering the place that you burn. How can you resolve such a difficulty?

Well, ask yourself—who will be seen? Perhaps it will be you. It could be you, wearing the clothes that you have always worn. It could also be you wearing a disguise. What is better than either of those two things?

Here is the best thing to do: arrange to begin a new life for yourself that is disconnected from the life that you have hitherto led. You will go away. You will know no one that you previously knew. You will use a new name. You will live by a skill that you previously did not display. Then, when you go to set your fire, you go as yourself, as you always go, in the costume you always wear. Then, the person who is discovered is you, but only the one you have been in the past. That person, insomuch as he/she may be found in the world, by her habits, by her dress, by her occupation, by her circle, no longer exists. There are biological traces that you will need to be careful not to leave—but this single precaution I speak of (and it is, I know, a difficult one to adopt) can help to ensure that you live your life happily undiscovered by the law.

A new ethic wherein people of any city, of any place, welcome itinerants with gentleness and secrecy could go a long way toward making this measure quite simple for anyone to adopt.

CIVILIAN OR MILITARY

The governments of the world would like very much for you to make the distinction between civilian and military targets. This is interesting because they do not make that distinction when they wage their class warfare upon us. Is a family a military target when they are beaten and thrown in the street and their belongings are tossed in the gutter? There are no military targets. Likewise, there are no civilian targets. These are abstract ideas that are part of a nineteenth-century framework. We are not sitting with frock coats at a Geneva Convention talking about war as the wealthy would like to wage it (on the backs of the poor). We are not talking about the war that is convenient for them.

I will say it again—we are here to help the mass of human beings who are under the thumb of some of the worst and most comprehensive oppression that has ever been devised. If we allow ourselves to be discovered in this, we shall be imprisoned, even killed.

And yet we shall continue!

FINAL NOTE

Do not be in a hurry. Remember—there is all of your life prior to the great fire you will set, and all of your life thereafter. That transition will require grace, thoroughness, and a deep compassion that stiffens into an unbreakable resolve. If it takes you some years to become the person who can burn a building, so be it. Carry your matches in your pocket, look at the faces of those who surround you in the crowd. Are we not all the same? Do we not all strive to simply have enough?

HALL

It was early—just before school. The hall had that feeling, like an empty train station. Any second this empty space would be packed with people and whatever was comforting about it would vanish.

I'd just printed the pamphlets out at the multimedia lab (on thick gray-colored paper)—which is the reason I was there early to begin with.

You can imagine how proud I was—I mean, I had never written a pamphlet before, not once in my life! And there I was, standing with them in my hand. Up walks Stephan and he asks me how the fire went. Of all the people. I was hoping not to see him.

I figured he'd ask, but I wasn't prepared—not while I was holding my pamphlet! Also—what a jackass, to say that shit out loud. But, I guess his pride was hurt and he wasn't thinking.

When I saw his pasty face, all I could think of was:

Can you imagine—to just go home when someone tells you to? Some people are soft all the way through, like a stick of butter.

That's what I mean about accomplices. Wise up. No one is ever careful enough.

How did the fire go?

He said it in this nasty way that I'm sure you would have expected (now that you have gotten to know him a little), as if it were my fault that he ran off like a pussy when Jan told him to.

I shoved the pamphlets in my bag.

I didn't go.

You didn't go?

Listen, I'm too busy for that shit. It's pretty immature anyway. Are you going to keep doing it? That guy seems like an asshole.

Yeah, I know he is. I grew up with him.

Lana came up just then and it was perfect.

She looked at Stephan with a bit of a sneer.

Hey, Lana, he said.

She looked at me, looked at him in mock horror, put her hand up to block the sight of him and asked me if he was gone yet.

I whispered, no, he's still here.

Damn it to hell, Stephan, she said. Know when you're wanted. Know when you're not wanted. It's a crucial skill.

He looked at me like I was going to stick up for him.
No way!

He shrugged.

Later, Lucia, he said and walked off.

Lana pretended to throw up on the carpet.

So, he's into you, huh. That's too bad.

Why?

Because I would never let you hang out with that guy.
Do you hang out with him? You don't do you?

No.

Is he your boyfriend? Do you lie under him on his family
couch? Do you have a visceral sense of how much he
weighs when he's on top of you?

Ugh, Lana, stop.

I would rather we both date my cousin. Matter of fact—
reason I'm standing here. We've got something on for
tonight. You're coming. No choice.

She stalked off down the hall. I realized she was wearing
pajamas and slippers. What a badass.

MEANING

A question I ask myself: what does it mean to make a pamphlet like that?

I am just starting my career as an arsonist, so you could say that it is my first entry in the field of arson, as a theorist. Right now I am a theoretical arsonist. Soon, I will be a theoretical and practical arsonist. Whatever Jan says about me being in the club now, I think it's nonsense. Both sides of the coin—I don't want any favors. If I am in the club it's because I started a fire. And I haven't done that.

That means, now the thing to do is for me

to set a really big fire.

The question is, what will I burn down, and how will I get away with it.

I have to make my plans.

First thing to do was: steal some sheets of paper from the art room. I guess steal is a bit of an exaggeration. The art teacher is a sweetheart with me—I don't have to steal the paper. She just gives it to me.

> *Paper.*
> *Pencil.*
> *Straightedge.*

Drawing board (to be returned).
Compass (to be returned).

For those of you who haven't got the first idea about how to do a thing right—this is the way. You get some paper and you plan the whole business, right from the get-go. You don't expect that things will happen perfectly—of course not. But, you end up better situated than some jackass who never thinks ahead. Or, you should. I guess there's no guarantee even of that.

By the way, they found the guy who started the music room fire. It was the fat guy, Ray, who I heard mention the Sonar Club that first time, the guy from detention. I know because I had to go to the office to get permission to leave school early to visit my mom, and he was there with his family. He was wearing a suit, like graduation or something. That's when I knew—Ray is gone for good.

If they make you put on a suit, it's because they are going to do something horrible to you, I guarantee it.

THE HOME

I won't go through my whole prediction rag this time.
This visit was kind of a catastrophe. I went to the Home.
I was sitting at the fish pond with my mom and she had an
accident. It seemed like she did, because she made a weird
expression, so I checked, and yes, an accident. I had to
get some help. Which meant going to the nurses' station.
When I got to the nurses' station he was there and he
came over.

I had to tell him that my mom had an accident, and would
he come clean it up.

Can you imagine?

Well, he did it. My good old mom got a towel bath from
the orderly who, well, you remember.

I don't think it mattered to her. I think it happens pretty
regularly. I tried to help him out, but he said he has
his routine for doing it—and it wouldn't take long. He
said I could walk around and he'd be done in about ten
minutes. I guess he didn't want me to watch him do it,
which is a little weird, since it is fairly high value—
I mean evolutionarily speaking, if you see that a guy
can do tasks like that, it probably makes you think he
would be a good mate. But, I don't think he thinks
like that. He probably thinks: I don't want her to
watch me clean shit off her mother's leg. Which makes
sense, too.

I came back and things were good as new. My mom was in her chair again. He was sitting there doing nothing. I guess he was waiting for me.

I asked him what his name was, which is something I didn't know. He told me. I told him my name. He said he knew it already, Lucia, it wasn't the kind of name you forget.

I told him you can forget anything.

AUNT

My aunt said she wasn't sure about the part where people get burned in their homes just for being wealthy. I said, there's no other way. They could have stopped at any time. She said, I know, but I'm still not sure about that part. In any case, I will be dead soon, and then the world will be yours to do with as you will.

Don't talk like that.

I like the rest, though, she said. I think maybe it is too formal. It should be simpler—like a person speaking to herself under her breath.

I said, the next one will be better.

PILLS

Lana said it was Ree's birthday and we were going to go
get her from her brother's shop where she works. We drove
over, and I got to ride in the front of the car for the first
time.

It's not mine, really, she told me. It's my brother's but he's
in jail. He would kill me, actually wring my neck if he knew
I had it.

What is your brother in jail for?

Mail fraud.

Really.

No, not really. He was in the coast guard and he got in
a fight while drinking. Unfortunately the guy he fought
had a heart condition.

Are you saying . . .

Yeah, he tackled the guy and that was that. So, he's in jail
until I'm twenty-five. He'll be thirty-two. Maybe he'll get
out on good behavior. He's a nice guy. Everyone was real
surprised.

We got to Ree's brother's place pretty quick (does he kill
people too? *No, Lucia. He doesn't. Only my brother kills
people, and he only kills people with heart conditions*),

which was an auto shop. There was a Ferrari logo on the outside.

He's never fucking seen a Ferrari, was Lana's comment on that.

Ree came out, tossed her bag in the back, and got in. She leaned in between us.

Hello, girls.

Hello, Ree.

Here you go. She handed us each two pills.

What is this?

That's the fun, said Lana. Ree never tells you what it is until after.

WHAT

DID

WE

DO

?

WHAT DID WE DO

The next day, I woke up and my face hurt. When I got to school, I passed by Lana in the hall and she had a black eye just like me.

Have you ever had a black eye before?

No. You?

No. Does it look cool?

It doesn't not look cool. I think it is—it could go either way.

We tried to put two and two together, but it was all real patchy. Lana called Ree at lunch, and Ree said we had done almost nothing. Lana put the phone on speaker:

Let's see. We got milkshakes at some diner. We drove past a carnival and went in and snuck into the bouncy castle, and when we were jumping around, the two of you knocked heads. You both fell on your asses, and bounced around. I have it on my phone, she said. I'll show you later. It is the funniest thing I have ever seen. You both thought it was your own fault and kept apologizing. Then we went to the bridge and listened to the radio and danced around for a while in the headlights of the car. It was the best birthday I have ever had. Lucia, you kept talking about how you can't get rid of your chlamydia.

I told her I knew that part wasn't true. To be honest,
I can't even remember thc difference between chlamydia
and gonorrhea. Is one of them worse?

THAT EVENING

He (Jan) said we'd need to stop by his house first, so we drove there. I was going to wait in the car, but he said I might as well come inside. It was a pretty crappy house, far back on a run-down property. I think they used to call this type a bungalow, but if it used to be a bungalow, I don't think anyone would call it that now.

I asked him,

Do you own this?

It was my grandfather's. Now, it's no one's.

The door was unlocked. We went in. There were empty beer cans here and there—it looked like a college house.

My room's back here.

I shrugged, like, why are you telling me where your room is.

Come on back, he said, and kept walking, so I followed.

His room was at the back of the house on the second floor. I guess it had been some kind of den. There was a bar at one end. Maybe his grandfather had liked entertaining guests. The room was actually pretty neatly kept. It didn't look like Jan owned very much.

He was changing his shirt, and I saw that he had scars.
I mean, Jan has a lot of scars.

That is a lot of scars, I said. He told me about them—where
they came from. It wasn't any one thing—and it wasn't
abuse, if that's what you were thinking. They were just
scars, just lots of scars.

What are we going to do? I asked after a while.

We're going to shoot a dog.

I won't do that, I said.

I'm joking. We are going to steal some potassium nitrate
from a farm supplier.

Can't you just buy it?

You can, but then your name might be on a list. Can't be
too careful.

We got back in his car. I realized I left my hoodie in his
room, so I ran inside to get it. I saw a photograph of a girl
on a ledge next to the bed.

When I got back to the car I asked him about her.

Forget about her, is what he said.

What if I don't?

She's my sister. She killed herself when I was eight.

Why?

It was an accident. She was holding her breath at the bottom of a pool.

I didn't say, I'm sorry, or anything like that—because I know it just pisses people off. I kept my mouth shut, he kept his mouth shut, and we drove for about another forty minutes. Once we stopped at a gas station for about two minutes. He went in, got a bottle of water, came out, and gave it to me.

In thirty seconds, we're going to pass by Revo's Supplies. I'm going to pull into the lot just past. That's an aquarium supply shop. You will get out. I will get out. You will go across the lot and into Revo's Supplies. There should be only one guy on duty. I want you to chat him up. I want you to ask him dumb questions about hammers and ratcheting tools versus nonratcheting tools and which you should get. Tell him some story about how your dad was a carpenter but died and you are going to get rid of his tools because you don't know what to do with them or how valuable they are. Make up some stories and run them. About a mile south on this road there's a taco shack. Meet me there in an hour.

We passed by a box building—red metal with a flat overhanging roof.

it said R E V O S P L Y.

Then we pulled into the next lot.

Get out.

I started getting out.

Hold on. Leave the sweatshirt.

No.

Then at least take it off. You need his attention, got it?

Yeah, I got it.

Revo's Supplies was a big store. The aisles were big, the counters were big, the ceiling was high. There was actually a tractor inside it, which was okay to look at. I went to the back, where there was a big counter. At the middle of the counter was a little hammer and a bell. RING ME, it said.

I rang it.

After about ten seconds, I rang it again. Then again and again.

A guy came out of the back wearing coveralls.

Hey, hey, stop that.

If you don't want people to ring the bell, don't have such a nice bell.

What do you need?

I need some screws for my air conditioner. The screws fell out. Now it doesn't fit in the window properly.

Do you know which screws those are? The screws are over here.

We went down one aisle a ways.

I don't know which ones they are.

Not sure what to tell you. Best bet would be—measure it and see? Or get the tech specs for the AC unit. I bet they're on the manufacturer's site.

Oh, yeah. Well, I need some other stuff too.

What can I do for you?

I was thinking about building a drafting desk, so I need to figure out what pieces of wood would be good, what kind, whether to use screws or nails, you know.

That's not really what we do here—I mean, I, hold on.

Another customer came in.

They knew each other and began to exchange pleasantries. I could tell the attendant wanted me to get the fuck out of his hair, so I pretended to look real hard at some kind of doorknob kit.

One second, miss.

He went over to the other guy.

I hung out for a few minutes to make sure enough time would pass to put Jan in the clear, then I took off.

The walk along the road to the taco shack was—scenic.
There were a lot of fields, another gas station, some kind of
small factory with Chinese characters on it, and a bunch of
Chinese guys sitting outside smoking. I bummed a cigarette
and smoked it with them. Would you believe not a single
one spoke English? I mean—they knew how to say hello,
but when I asked what county or town we were in, they
couldn't say. I heard about this once, that sometimes people
will move a whole town to the U.S. There is a town in a
different country, and the whole town moves here,
and takes up residence. Then, they don't really need to
speak English. I think that's great. Fuck English. If I grew
up next to a Laotian village, maybe I'd speak two languages
already, instead of one and a half.

The taco shack, as far as I could tell, was out of business.
Jan was waiting in the parking lot, though, and he flashed
his brights at me from about a quarter mile away.

When I got in he said, I wasn't going to mention it, but you
know you look like a fucking raccoon. Who did that to you?

STICKER

In the car, I showed him a sticker Lana and I had made on her computer. We were going to have a bunch printed up so we could put them around.

You made that? he said.

Yeah, well, Lana did a lot of it. We both did it.

Right.

He didn't say anything for a while.

Do you know whose coffin that is?

DO YOU KNOW WHOSE COFFIN IT IS?

Lana and I kind of had an argument about the meaning of the sticker. She said that it was just a basic anarchist sticker, whatever that means. I said it is more complicated because of whose coffin it is. Now, I'm the one who picked out the photograph, so I didn't expect her to know whose coffin it was, but then it turned out she did know. Apparently she liked outlaws when she was a kid.

The guy in the coffin is Jesse James. They are showing off his body after he has been killed because his celebrity was such that you became more important just by being in a photograph with his corpse. So, for someone who is walking down the street and sees the sticker: they are selling coffins, you know—you think you are buying something that is useful to you, but it is just a weight on you. It is as useless to you as a coffin. And why is a coffin useless to you? Because when you climb in it you're already dead.

POLICE

Next day, I get off the bus by the house and there's a police car there waiting for me.

What is it, officer?

(No reason not to be polite.)

Lucia Stanton?

They took me back to the precinct and asked me a whole bunch of questions. They showed me a picture of Jan and asked if I knew him. I said I couldn't tell. The picture was bad. It could be anyone. They asked if I knew some other people, a guy named Lance, a girl named Willa.

I don't know them. Do you?

I know who they are. Why do you think I'm asking you?

How did you get my name anyway?

Someone said you knew these people. Someone you know.

A lot of people think they know me.

I bring out the worst in people, but in this case, after a while, the cops and me, we got along. I can get along with anybody. They wanted to know who hit me, and I explained about getting high as fuck and going in the bouncy castle with my two cute girlfriends. They liked that quite a lot, maybe too much. They had me tell it twice and the second time one of them asked me what we were wearing. What do you mean? *What were you wearing in the bouncy castle?* Some of the other officers gave that guy a look and he shut up.

I didn't even have to take the bus home, because one of them was going that way and gave me a ride home.

I felt like I had really tricked them, but when the officer let me out, he said,

Lev told me to tell you, friendly advice, it costs nothing: stay away from those people. You don't know what they're like.

This is you being a sweetheart, I said.

That's right.

EVENTS

Sometimes events speed up. You think you have a handle on them. You think you understand how one thing follows another, but then it turns out you can't even perceive what is about to happen, and before you know it, not only that, but other things too—they all have happened, and you're standing in the rubble trying to figure out what to do.

I started wanting to go to school less and less. I was hanging out with Lana and her cousin and Jan more and more. I started to feel any request that was made on me was too much.

When people write books about childhood, and about being a kid—they always talk about how endless it is, and about how there is no thought of time. Everything just stretches and stretches. I think the opposite is the case. When you're young, you feel like things are constantly ending. As soon as you get used to something, it goes away. There was an old couple who used to watch me when I was four or five, and I would go into their backyard. There was a low part and a high part as the yard rose up a hill, and on the high part, kind of a trail, I guess, there were flowers—just an endless path of flowers and white stones. I know that when I was there, when I was four and I was there on that path, I felt sure that life was almost over. I felt like most of it had already come and gone. I don't think I even knew about death yet.

HOUSE

My aunt says that I am naturally curious. That means that I don't need to be taught how to learn. Some people have a disadvantage at the beginning, and they are not curious. These people have trouble learning. It seems like not being curious is the worst thing of all. Curious people aren't necessarily good at learning what you want them to learn, though. They are too busy learning about other things.

My aunt said to me, while we were sitting in the garden, let's go into the house. So, we went into the house.

Then, we were in the house, and she said, let's go back out to the garden, I was wrong.

So, we went back out into the garden.

There's a thing I have to tell you, she said. I think this is it. I pretty much think this is it.

What do you mean?

I want us to go back inside in a bit and I will sit down in my chair, and you can sit near me. Maybe make some tea. I think this may be, I think it may be it.

I started crying, but with no sound. I could see she didn't like it, so I got myself together and stopped. It was like trying to swallow something enormous, something made out of air, and I couldn't do it, but then I did.

I helped her back inside, and got her into the chair. She started telling me a bunch of things she was sorry about, and how she wished that she was younger, how she even wished we could be the same age, because we matched up so well, and how she was proud of me, so proud, it was like I was her daughter. I said, stop it. She said, I will, I will.

I held her hand, and after a while gave her the tea. She held the cup for a second and then I took it back and put it on the ground by the chair.

Why don't you put on a record, she said. Something quiet. I said okay, I'll put on a record. I'll go do that.

I found a record. I put it on.

I came back across the room, and behind me the record was just starting, behind me there was hissing and hissing and as the first few notes came, scratched out of the dark plastic by the needle, I looked for her in the chair where her body was, but I saw that she wasn't there.

WENTWORTH

The Wentworth building stands at the end of a big avenue. You can see it from a mile away. Matter of fact, it's like the hand of a clock, because when the sun is shining on some parts of town, other parts get nothing because they are in its shadow.

I decided I was done with people. Even good ones—they can't do much for you.

Lana and I pretended to be going to some office, and we got to the roof of the Wentworth building. The elevator doesn't even go all the way. The last five floors are these majestic stairs. I guess it was a place for captains of industry or some other hateful types. This beautiful staircase comes to a huge double door that is cobwebbed and dirty. I kicked at it and Lana rammed it. Then we saw there was another door on the side. We kicked at that, and kicked at it. It opened and we got out onto the roof.

The sudden expanse was—surprising. The thing about distance is, it feels complete. Maybe it is the opposite of complete, but it feels so finished in its endlessness.

We walked out toward the edge.

Wait.

I'm not afraid, I said.

Afraid of what? Wait up.

I walked right to it, as if I were walking on a sidewalk.
I mean, my toes were hanging over. My body swayed
forward, then back, then forward. I looked down, and
I felt nothing.

Asshole, get back here.

No, you come over here.

I sat down with my legs hanging off. The roof was warm,
real warm, and I could feel the warmth all through my
legs. The breeze was stiff and cool, and it came now and
then.

Lana crept to the edge and sat next to me.

You asshole.

We looked down over the town.

It is so hard, she said, to take it seriously. Matter of fact,
I refuse to. Long as I live, I won't take anything seriously.
What do you say?

I said I would agree, for me and for my aunt, too.

Lana was quiet for a while.

She's dead, isn't she?

Yeah. How'd you know?

Your eyes are swollen. Was it yesterday?

Yeah.

Crazy old bat. I don't want to live that long.

Me neither.

I want to die in the afternoon—when it's just stopped raining and no one's around.

How would you do it?

I would walk out into the middle of a public park, some beautifully trimmed lawn. People would be starting to leave their houses. From every direction they'd be coming toward me, but they wouldn't be there yet. Because by the time they got there, they would find that I was dead. No matter when they did come, I would just be a corpse in a park.

. . .

We sat for a while.

What would you do? she asked me.

I think I would go to the top of a building with a friend, and then I would leap off, jump all the way to the ground and be crushed against it. The ground isn't dangerous. It's just the ground, but somehow when I touched it, I would be crushed against it. No matter how delicately I reached out my hands, my feet, I would be crushed flat.

Shut the fuck up. Do it then.

Oh, we laughed and laughed, Lana and me.

Everyone should just crush themselves to death.

Yeah, everyone should do that. Why not?

I can't think of a reason.

Wait, wait. No. No, I can't either.

Let's throw something off.

Like what?

To sum up, let me tell you: I'm not one of those nihilistic types who thinks there is no meaning. I guess, I don't think there's meaning; there's definitely no meaning, but not in a nihilistic way. I don't find it exciting the way they do. I think you could as well be a bug or a sparrow or part of an antler, or the back of someone's pocketknife.

There's a story someone told me, a friend of my aunt's who came to the funeral. She said, your aunt was at the soup kitchen and a guy came in and he wanted a bowl of soup, but there wasn't any soup. We call it a soup kitchen, but more often there are sandwiches, or burritos or whatever. Soup is kind of messy. But he wants some soup. So, my aunt gets him a sandwich and she sticks it in his bowl and hands it to him with a spoon and she says, soup for one. Apparently all the people at the shelter liked this a lot. They would always say, soup for one. Soup for one. One guy even tattooed it on his leg. Can you imagine? That you can say something, offhand, and it can matter, it can really matter to someone else? Can you imagine what it's like to hear something like that? To hear someone say something and feel the world ripple around you?

LETTER

Well, I got back to my aunt's place, and I stood there looking around. It felt pretty bad, I have to say, being in a place like that. I stuck most of my things in an army bag and put it by the door. That made me feel a little better. Then I noticed an envelope that was on the kitchen table. Somehow I hadn't seen it.

—LUCIA—

It was addressed to me—a letter from my aunt. She must have left it out the day before. She was probably waiting for me to find it. That's the kind of thing she would do—and did, all the time.

I opened it. There were two letters inside. One was from Hausmann. It was an acceptance letter.

I sank into the chair. Then I realized I was sitting in the chair where my aunt died and I started to stand up. But, I decided, why not. I might as well huddle there with her death, so I curled up and looked at the other letter.

It was from my aunt. One thing about her that you should know—her handwriting is perfect. It looks like the work of a Victorian handwriting machine. She writes on paper without lines and all the words are perfectly laid down, everything symmetrical. I think it has to do with her posture.

Anyway—this is what she said:

LETTER

Lucia, dear girl,

It is of course your decision and I will respect whatever it is that you choose to do. However, you should know that opportunities do not come so easily as the years pass, and that therefore, when one is young, it can be a savvy choice to obtain what you may as freely as you may. If these people will house you and give you a place to grow—you do not even need to learn what they want you to learn. You can continue your own education in the midst of these circumstances, which, you must admit, appear quite lovely. It is also true that you might find people there to talk to. It is always a pleasure to have people to talk to, people of real worth. We have always had each other, but I am sure that you will soon be alone—and then what?

However any of this might be, I want you to know that I am quite overcome with pride—not that you have managed to be admitted to this school, but that you have not failed to be the person I have always hoped you would be. It is a sad thing for me that I imagine I will not live to see you become utterly her—become her whom you will be inalienably. That person, I feel, will be someone to behold.

Goodbye for now,

Your strongest supporter always,
Lucy

LETTER

Well, I cried for a while, I don't mind saying. I folded
the letter up and stuck it in my pocket. The one from
Hausmann I put in my bag. I stood up and looked around
the room and it was as if I had never seen it before. My
eyes moved over the various objects and I truly felt at that
moment as if I had never seen any of them, as if I was for
a moment, entirely new. I wondered what I would do.

That's when I noticed it. On the back wall—something was
missing. My aunt basically owned nothing, you know that
already. But, she did have an old wedding dress and an old
suit and the old wedding dress and the old suit, they hung
together on the back wall of the house—like a costume
exhibit. Next to the old wedding dress and next to the old
suit there was a framed picture. In the picture, there were
two people. One of them was a man. He was wearing the
suit, but in the picture it was not an old suit. The other
was a woman, a pretty young woman, and in the picture
she was wearing the wedding dress. That woman was
my aunt.

The picture was gone; the dress was gone; the suit was
gone. There wasn't even any reason for someone to take
that stuff—some useless old clothes. It had to have been
just some creepy whim.

But, I was pretty sure I knew who had done it.

Next thing I knew, I was on the front steps. I banged
on the glass. Nothing. I banged on the glass. Nothing.

The landlord came to the door. Maybe I mentioned him to you before. 1. He hates me. 2. He hates me.

He opened it, looked down at me. I could tell he knew I knew.

What do you want?

There was just enough room, so I brushed past him into the house.

I know what you did.

He yelled at me to stop, but I ran into the next room, I guess it was the kitchen. There, on the counter, I saw it in a big pile—right there on the counter he'd stuck the dress and the suit and the framed photo.

Asshole!

I grabbed the stuff from the counter and turned around. He stood there, blocking my way.

He said something about my aunt owing him money.

I said the clothes weren't worth anything anyway. He'd better let me go.

He threatened to call the police.

So I put down the stuff. I could see that he thought he'd won. His expression changed, and became if anything, even uglier. The wreck that age had made of his face, which is usually something I like to see—I admire it—in this case made him look like a vile clown. His mouth was practically spitting at me in his supposed victory:

Now get out of here, he said.

I went to go by him and he grabbed my shoulder. I tried to get him off, but he pulled me along and tossed me out the door.

I ran back to the garage and just sat there sobbing like a weak little wretch. For some reason it was too much for me. Someone like my aunt, she venerates this stupid clothing that she wore a million years ago, just because her life is a train wreck and for her sometimes thinking back on one of the few good things, her ultimately fruitless wedding, could make her feel good—and what happens? When she's dead, even this dumb little display of her ordinariness— even that doesn't get respected. It gets taken by the landlord who likes collecting quaint worthless shit. I wonder how long he had his eye on it.

I felt right then that I needed to get as far away as possible from this, from the beginnings of my life. If I could get some distance away, I was sure I could make something clean and cold and clear. Someplace else, not here, I could be the inheritor of my aunt's, my father's ideas.

Two minutes later, I heard the sirens.

A minute after that, the noise came: people in the garden.

Someone was saying something, maybe the landlord's nephew.

Another voice said, we'll take care of it. Just hang back.

Then another voice: hang back.

There was a knock at the door. I went over and opened it. There must have been ten people out there.

Turns out the old man was claiming I shoved him and threatened his safety inside his own house. I don't remember it that way, but I guess it could have happened.

LANA

Next thing you know, I was sitting with Lana in her
car outside the police station. My duffel bag was in the
back with what I guess was everything I own. I was
filling Lana in on what happened:

What happened was this:

The old man claimed I was trespassing. I thought
he meant trespassing in his house when I went to get
the wedding dress. Not so. He meant trespassing by
being on the property. Turns out he had already filed
a complaint against my aunt and me, just in case, for
squatting in his garage. They pulled that out and it
looked pretty bad. So, presto—that was that. The
police officer told me the old man would drop the
charges if I'd stay away. I said I would and that was
that. When I started to talk about the wedding dress,
which I did, I mean, I really started giving a shitty little
speech, everyone shut up for a second in that part of
the precinct, and that's when I realized that I sounded
totally fucking crazy. A wedding dress from 1940?
Who cares? So, I stopped talking and walked out
and no one stopped me. I guess I had already been
processed.

Ten minutes later, Lana picked me up. I told her my
side of the story and we drove away. She was madder
than I was. In general I think sadness kind of takes the
strength away from anger, or maybe they just waver

back and forth. I don't know. All I know is most of the time I am one or the other—that is, angry or sad. We get offered so few real victories. It's a question I can't even really answer: what is the victory I want?

MONDAY

That was a Friday. The fallout didn't come until
Monday. Over the weekend, I tried to sneak back
into my aunt's to get a few more things, but there were
new locks on the door. I stayed at Lana's the first night,
then at Jan's Saturday and Sunday. Monday I went
to school.

I got pulled straight out of homeroom and sent to the
principal's. Of course, I know that terrible room pretty
well by now. What I didn't know was, the principal
evidently knew someone who knew my aunt's landlord.
I guess everybody I hate knows each other, like some
kind of club.

So, in a thirty-minute harangue I was told by the
principal, who was red-faced (he even swore three
or four times), that he was going to make damned well
sure nothing went well for me at the school going
forward and that I should consider dropping out. Matter
of fact, I should more than consider it. He said he didn't
have the power to kick me out, but he could make it
tough for me if I stayed, and he would.

I headed for the door.

I'm not done, he said.

I told him he could fuck himself.

He said something like: he could see my whole life stretched out—failures and failures and failures. We tried to help you, he said. But you can't be helped.

That was enough for me.

GOODBYE WHISTLER

And there I was, standing in the hall. Let's not be romantic about it. I hated the place from the get-go. And so, that was the end of my sojourn at Whistler High.

Nothing left for me to do but take the licorice I'd socked away in my locker, toss my textbooks on the ground, and waltz out the grand front entrance like I owned it. So, I did that. The hallway felt enormous, I don't know why. It's almost like—we don't see things most of the time, but every now and then, BAM—your sight gets defamiliarized, and then everything looks new, like you've never seen it before.

A few kids were trailing in late to first period, and I could see they were confused by my behavior. A teacher tried to stop me—asked where I was going.

I just laughed.

That didn't go over well.

Listen, either you're a student or you're not. And if you're not a student anymore you can't be on school grounds.

I get that. I get it. That's why I'm walking this way. Do you see what direction this is?

The people at Whistler High are a real mixed bag.

I crossed the street, and went up into the woods a bit.
I'd thought about going up into those woods for a while,
but I had never done it. There were some fallen trees and
I sat down on one. From where I sat I could see the whole
high school building opposite. Different scenes were
framed in all the windows, and along the arterial of the
front drive, cars came and went. The whole thing was a
vulgar facsimile of something useful, but a false version,
one that does no good. Imagine if someone would show you
a beehive that doesn't make honey. What's the point of it,
you say? Oh, it's just to keep the bees busy. We love it when
they learn to like what's given to them. That's what the
voice would say if it decided to reveal itself to you.
But usually it keeps quiet.

LANA

The next day, Lana came to Jan's place and told me
Beekman wanted me to call him. She gave me his phone
number on a piece of paper.

I don't really like him, she said, but he seemed pretty mad
at the principal, so I guess he's all right.

Weird. I don't really know why it matters so much to him.

Don't ask me.

Can I use your phone to call?

Lana said we needed to get me my own phone. I said didn't
I know it.

The phone rang for a while, then Beekman answered:

1. He was sorry about my aunt dying. I said it was probably
the best thing for her, which is essentially meaningless, but
I discovered it is a good way to end conversations like that.

2. He was mad at me for quitting school. He said the
principal was bluffing about ruining things for me there.
There isn't much a principal can do even if the principal
hates you, he said. The teachers wouldn't stand for him
just victimizing students. I said, what's done is done.
I wasn't learning anything anyway. He didn't say anything
to that.

3. He asked if I had been arrested for assaulting an old man in his home. I said it was complicated and gave him my account of things, which basically took forever. Lana kept shaking her head at me.

4. I asked him if the principal had called Hausmann. He said it had happened and that now it looked like I couldn't go. They were *very hesitant to take on a high-risk individual.* He was really disappointed in them.

5. He said his wife and he had talked and if I needed a place to stay, they would help me out. He said he knew my situation was rough and I shouldn't give up on myself. I said I had a place, but thank you.

6. He said he and his wife would like to help me. He said again, I could stay with them and potentially do a GED. Then, he was sure I could get into a great college. I said I couldn't talk anymore, but I'd think about it.

LANA

I was standing there holding Lana's phone. The call was over. I said, I'm through with having people try to help me out.

What's wrong?

I guess I'm not going to that fancy school.

It's not so bad. That means we can keep hanging out.

Yeah.

I mean—if they get into you for something like this, maybe it was a bad idea anyway.

I just wish . . .

I felt pretty awful. Maybe I even started to screw up my face a little like I was going to cry.

Lana looked over. She started to mock me.

That goddamned landlord. He really did a job on you. All he has to do is call the police and no matter what happened, you're fucked.

Lana grabbed my head in both her hands and looked into my eyes.

Now you're completely screwed. You poor child, now you can never accomplish anything.

Fuck off.

I tried to shake her, but she had my head real good.

Now there's nothing left for you. Why don't you cry some more?

Fuck off, Lana.

Cry little baby, cry. You don't get to go to your fancy school.

Lana! Stop.

No, no I won't. You're the one who has to stop being a little bitch.

She stuck her forehead right against mine.

Nobody knows what you can do. Nobody knows that.

She pushed me away.

Surprise them. Do whatever you want. They don't matter anyway. It's like you keep telling me—they're all stuck in their own heads.

Thanks, Lana.

Lucia, you are a foul bitch—not a sucker. Keep to the script.

Have you been reading my pamphlet?

Are you kidding? I memorized it.

MOTHERS

We went on a walk then, after Lana's pep talk. There is a sump about a half mile from Jan's house and we walked down there. Some guys honked at us from a car and drove slowly next to us; Lana gave them the finger and they laughed. Evidently that was what they liked, so they started to pull over. We went into a torta shop and waited until they went away.

We were staring out the window. I was thinking about boys and how terrible it must be to be a boy. They seem to feel like they have to stand up to everything, and for no reason.

The cashier at the torta place asked us if we were going to order anything, so we got up and left.

Just then Lana asked me about my mom. She did it this way, like she was far down her train of thought, and it somehow jumped straight out into speech:

What kind of bullshit is that? Tell me, please.

What are you talking about?

Our conversations. They are like this: I say something about my mom. You say nothing. I say something about my dad. You say nothing. I tell you about my brother. You say nothing. So, the question is: what kind of bullshit is that?

Lana, what do you want me to say?

Why haven't you taken me to see your mom? You go there every week. I don't mind going with you.

Maybe I mind.

Nobody said anything for a while and I could tell she was hurt—and here's the thing, I like Lana. I don't want her to feel bad. Basically, she is near the end of the line of people I wouldn't mind seeing hurt, and it's a long line.

Lana, listen. My mom, you would have liked her a lot. You would have. But there's nothing to like now. Going there—you're not going there to see a person. It isn't like that.

Why don't you tell me about her then?

Fine. I told her a story:

She was really wild. Sometimes she didn't care about consequences. She and my aunt would argue about this a lot. My dad was pretty crazy too, but he was the one who kept my mom in check. Once, they were sitting in a diner, and I was with them. I was maybe eight. Some guy pulled up in a truck and he went inside real quick, he left the truck running. We paid, and he was still in line as we were leaving. The back of the truck is full of Christmas trees. My mom says hurry up to my dad. They jump in the truck, me on my dad's lap, and we peel out. My mom drives it full speed down to this one neighborhood, a pretty bad spot, and we dump all the Christmas trees onto a lot, drive to a spot under an overpass. They left the truck there and we walked home in the cold, laughing and laughing and laughing. She never got caught. That was one thing about her, she never got caught.

So, that was one thing about her, one side of her. The other side was: she'd take the newspaper out and we'd sit down on Sundays and we'd go through it page by page finding lies and weasel words. It's pretty fun. We would compare the new paper with old ones. We would just laugh and laugh. My mom would do impressions, and different accents, trying out what the different articles said. It was one of my favorite things. Sometimes we would call my dad over to verify if we couldn't remember things, and he loved it, too. I think he wanted to do it with us, but he could see it was nice that we got to do it alone. Also, she would make cheesecake compulsively. I actually don't even like cheesecake.

Sounds like a pretty great family, said Lana. My mom doesn't know one end of a hot dog from the other.

She's sweet, though, I said. And she managed to not die or turn into a vegetable.

Lucia, come on. Don't say that.

If you saw her, Lana, if you saw her and she was your mom, it's the worst thing you could ever see.

I guess that made Lana feel bad. I shouldn't have said it, but the truth is the truth:

We're just not permanent at all, not the way we want to be. Something happens, maybe even something small, something no one even notices, and next thing you know someone is spooning porridge in your mouth and maybe you like it. Next thing you know someone is wheeling you into a room with carpeted walls.

FIRE

FIRE

FIRE

FIRE

FIRE

FIRE

FIRST

When we began, I bet you didn't think things would go this way, did you? I didn't think so either. When I look back, the girl I was at the outset was pretty helpless. I imagine I continue to be pretty helpless now. Helplessness: it's our essential condition with regard to the future, no?

The idea was: for the first couple of weeks I would stay sometimes at Jan's, sometimes at Lana's. I didn't have a plan beyond that.

Lana's mom was pretty angry that I quit school. I think this was mostly because it meant Lana was a hop skip and a jump from quitting school herself. Her mom had the misguided view that school was educating people for glorious and varied lives in a vivacious modern world. But, as my aunt would say—it's not my job to improve anybody. That meant instead of arguing with her I would just bring her little presents—some wildflowers or a rock or something I stole from the grocery store. Her tune changed from, Lucia should go back to school to Lucia has such good manners, Lana. Why don't you have manners like Lucia has? And that was fine with me.

Alternately, when I stayed at Jan's, things were pretty calm. He does different things to get money, I don't know what, so he is only there part of the time, and he doesn't care if I hang around. If there is food in the kitchen, I can eat it. Basically, he doesn't care. You can come up with your contribution later, he said.

So, what did I do all day if I wasn't at school and I had no job?

I sat around a bunch and wrote down things I could remember about my aunt. Ever since she first went to the hospital I have been writing down everything I could remember about this whole time—from when I got kicked out of the first school, right up until the present. That's what you've been reading, obviously. A person writes down what has happened in order to *know it*. Then a person can find the way forward.

I thought a lot too about my dad and what he would say. He might say something like: head out west hopping freight trains and be a labor organizer. He was a real romantic that way, my dad. Nowadays nobody cares like that. If you showed up at a construction site people would be too busy looking at their phones to listen to anything you might say. The problem has to be handled differently. But how?

So, I was thinking about stuff like that. Hausmann had maybe given me some false hopes, but now I was realizing: maybe I had made a mistake by believing in this ludicrous fantasy. Lucia, I said to myself sternly, you should believe in inevitable things. Anything else is frippery.

Oh, and there was still the matter of my aunt's funeral.

FUNERAL

My aunt hadn't gotten a real funeral. They just cremated
her one day. I wasn't even invited. There I was crying
my eyes out, expecting I would somehow know. I mean—
you imagine you will know when your own aunt's
funeral will be. But it isn't true. It's not like a cherub
flies through the sky and blows a horn for you.

When I went to the funeral home, they didn't have any
information. When I went to the church, they said it was
all over. I mean, all over, but it had never really happened.
They showed me a place where they put you if you have no
money for your own grave. It is essentially a garbage dump
for ashes.

So, what you're saying, I told the chaplain, is that she's
somewhere in there.

Yes.

Along with a bunch of other people.

Yes.

And dogs, cats, pets?

Oh, oh no—those go somewhere else entirely. I don't want
you to think that . . .

Oh, don't worry, I told him. Whatever it is you don't want
me to think, I'm not thinking it.

+

There was a certain correctness to the absolutely uneceremonious annihilation of my aunt's body. It is a kind of perfect finish for an atheist. Even I can't complain—it's not like I think my aunt was sticking around inside her own body.

Nonetheless, I wanted to have some kind of funeral for her. So, what I decided was this: the fire I was going to set, that would be my aunt's funeral. It would be a kind of homage to her and to the life I hoped to lead.

The question was—how would I do it?

JAN, LANA, LUCIA

Jan and Lana never agree. Whatever it is that we are
talking about doing, or planning, or arguing about,
they are always on one side and the other. I mean, one
is on one side, the other is on the other. This is funny
because most of the time I agree with both of them.
I'm almost positive they just disagree out of spite. In any
case, there is one thing that they both agreed about, and
it was this:

When we got to talking about the fire I was planning on
setting for my aunt's funeral, I mentioned, I mean it just
fell out of my mouth, that I wanted to burn the wedding
dress. Somehow, I felt it needed to be burned. If for my
aunt it represented her life, then it shouldn't stick around.
It just shouldn't.

That's when Lana said if I felt that way I should go burn it,
or I'd feel like a coward forever.

That's when Jan said: he took that dress and that suit—it
was like a little shrine to your aunt's life. If you want to give
her a funeral, burn it to the ground.

I said let's not get ahead of ourselves.

Jan said, he chose to take it into his house. He took it there.
For the funeral, all that you want to do is burn those things,
but if they are in his house . . . well, who chose to have
them there? It is pretty simple.

That's what I'm saying, said Lana.

When they said that, I felt somehow that it was right, just right.

The plan, then, was basic. I wasn't even mad at the landlord, not really. I was just sad and tired. It was like a signature. I was going to give this funeral like writing my signature in ash, and then I would get out of town. For such a long time I have wondered: what does a beginning look like? I said it out loud.

Maybe this, said Lana.

We have to make sure, I said, that he isn't in there.

That's easy, said Jan.

He'll just end up in the position that I'm in—having nothing.

I've got some of it right here.

Lana held my bag open.

Licorice and nothing!

You and your fucking licorice, said Jan.

The Hausmann letter was in there, though. I remembered it, and it suddenly bothered me. I pulled it out. I don't know why I had kept it until then, so I tore it in half.

More nothing. More and more and more. More nothing.
I threw the pieces on the ground and Lana and I danced
around on them. Why did we do that? What does it mean
to dance on something? I don't know. Obviously you can
dance for a reason, but sometimes I think we dance for
no reason at all.

STEPHAN

The next morning something unfortunate happened.
I was sleeping and I heard a knock on the door. I don't
know what day exactly it was—I guess Saturday. Jan
was off somewhere. I went down to see who it was. When
I got to the door and opened it, standing there in Jan's yard
before the busted bungalow was Stephan.

Stephan?

Lucia?

I hadn't seen him in a while—obviously.

What are you doing here?

Why are you wearing Jan's shirt?

What are you talking about? Do you want something?

He was really uncomfortable.

He just repeated himself.

What are you doing here?

Stephan, hello. Can I help you with something?

Tell Jan I came by. He asked me to.

Okay.

As he made his way across the yard, he kept looking
back. I almost felt like—I mean, I'm sure it wasn't true,
but I almost felt like he was crying, which is weird. Don't
you think?

When I told Jan about it later, he thought it was funny.
I forgot all about him, he said. I guess I did say he should
stop by, but the problem is, with a guy like him, you tell
him something like that, and then there is just no way you
can remember. You might even want to keep your word,
but you just cannot remember what you said to him. It is
all so non-notable.

GERTY

I was just leaving Green Gully—I had made it about forty feet down the sidewalk when I hear a voice calling my name. It was a close thing—I almost ran, and I'm sure you can guess why:

I had three boxes of licorice under my hoodie!

But, when I turned around, I saw that it was just some old lady from my aunt's church. I didn't know her name, so I decided to call her Gerty; that's what I did when I spoke to her.

You might ask why I would do that, well, here's the thought process: if she knows from the outset that I don't know her name, then she might want to wrap up the conversation sooner; if she decides to pretend that is her name and prolong the whole business, it makes the conversation funnier; if she decides to tell me what her real name is, then we have two options, a) real understanding, and b) I pretend to forget and call her Gerty again.

Now, mind you, I am always really nice to people, so none of this is like, Lucia is being mean to an old lady. It is just— well, I have had to have too many conversations like this in my life, and life is short. Anyway, when I talk to people like that, I am really nice. I look them right in the eye and smile for all I'm worth.

So, she comes up and says that my aunt died. I mean, I know that. What she says is—something about my aunt dying and how it relates to her. So be it. I am not that interested in that kind of thing. She asks me what I am going to do now. What are my plans now that I am alone?

I say that I am enrolled in a beauty academy and I am going to learn to do makeup really good. Then, I can be an "active part of it all." This is what I said.

Maybe she thought I was going to say something else. What I did say kind of took her off guard, and she was relieved. Evidently, she thought I had a lot of common sense, like, head screwed on right and all that.

I think she wanted to give me a hug, but I didn't want her to notice the licorice boxes under my sweatshirt, so I just made off.

THE PLAN

I wrote out the plan on a big sheet of paper. Lana sat next to me on the bed and watched. She was eating a donut.

She said, if I eat any more of these donuts I am going to be a fat shit and it will solve my donut problem because my boyfriend will dump me for being a fat shit and then I won't get any free donuts anymore. That's what they call a logical syllogism.

I laughed.

She said, see, I've been doing some reading of my own.

I said, that's not a syllogism. A syllogism would be like, All girls who eat donuts become fat girls. All fat girls stop eating donuts. Therefore all girls who eat donuts stop eating donuts.

That's what I'm saying, she said. The problem solves itself.

On one part of the paper I drew up the resources that we have:

A large house.
A garden (parts not visible from the street).
Lighters, matches.
Gasoline.
Pipe bombs.
Gunpowder.

Three workers.
Two cars.
Two phones (could get more).
Candles.
50m of fuse.
Electric detonator.

On another part I wrote in big letters:

IT WILL BE OBVIOUS WHO DID THIS SO YOU NEED TO
LEAVE TOWN IMMEDIATELY, LUCIA, DON'T THINK YOU
CAN GO ON LIVING AROUND HERE.

When I wrote that, Lana said quietly, maybe I'll go with
you.

Would you?

Maybe I would. Is there something better going on?

Her quiet was contagious. We were both quiet for a minute.

If we were going to get out of town, she said, we should
make arrangements ahead of time, that's for sure.

She looked over the piece of paper.

Lucia, you told me about all the junk he has piled in every
room of the goddamned place. It sounds like a firetrap
to me. You don't have that down as a resource. Don't you
think . . .

And with that—she had solved it.

I had forgotten a basic rule: if you want it to be simple, then make it simple. I could just light the room with the wedding dress and the whole place would go up.

I looked down at my nice plan with its diagrams and lists. I crossed them out.

Lana, a person could easily get to disliking you.

I know it, she said. Don't I know it.

JAN

Jan didn't come back that night, or the next. Lana and
Ree and I were sitting around and I said I was worried.
Lana said maybe he got run over by a tractor trailer. We
went down to his place, and it was wrecked. It looked like
someone had gone over it looking for something.

I said, if he got picked up by the police I don't want to go to
the station to check up on him. Probably not a good idea.
Lana said she wasn't the one to go either. We just both
looked at Ree for a while, because she can get anything she
wants out of a chump guy, and finally she buckled. She said
she'd be back in half an hour and she borrowed Lana's keys.

Half an hour passed and lights came in the driveway. Ree
said he was up in county. Evidently someone had been
telling stories about him, and when they tossed the house
they found all kinds of materials. He might be there a
while. I felt a little sick about it.

He's a sweetheart, for sure, said Ree.

Why?

He didn't put them on to you.

Lana chimed in to tell me how lucky I was that my things
were at her place by chance when the police raided Jan's.
And not just your things, but you. You're lucky you weren't
there.

But I didn't do anything yet.

Well, he didn't do anything either.

I don't know about that. Maybe he did.

Lucia, you're lucky you weren't there.

Yeah, I guess so. Here's to staying lucky.

We toasted with what was left of the plastic vodka bottle.

Ree did a little pirouette as we went back to the car. She stopped and dropped into a crouch looking up at us.

But who would have told on him? Do you have any guesses?

NOTE

Lana and I lay on her bed and talked late into that night.
She was excited as hell. She said it would be such a
surprise for her mom and for her boyfriend when she just
disappeared.

Won't you leave a note for your mom?

Yeah, oh fuck, I don't know. What do you think?

Even if it makes it a little worse for us, I think.

She deserves it, yeah. I guess so. But I'm not telling Hal.
It's not like he's going to have it rough finding a new
girlfriend.

I agreed. Plenty of them sniffing around him day and
night.

She got all businesslike suddenly.

So, tomorrow, we pack. You go to the Home. We buy
the bus tickets for the day after. Then we sleep for the last
time here.

That's right.

And what about Jan—do you think he will . . .

A guy like him—he has to take care of himself.

We lay there for a while. I don't know what she was thinking about, but I was thinking about Lucia Stanton— this person who would basically disappear. What would I call myself next? What clothes would I wear? There is that part in the Bardo Thodol where the dead person goes into a womb to be born again into a new place, where the dead person actually chooses where she will be born—whether into an animal or a human, and into which land. Now, I know that's just some Tibetan nonsense, but it is a good metaphor. So, I lay there thinking:

Who will you be, Lucia, when you are not Lucia anymore?

LAST BIT

I wrote down that last section after Lana went to sleep. From here on in, there isn't time to write things, so I will just put down my final prediction about how things will go, and then it'll be things as they come, however they come.

Two days from now, Lana and I will go down to the bus station. We will put our bags into a locker there. We will return to her mom's house. We will get a container of gasoline from the backyard where we hid it. Together, we will go in her brother's car to a spot some blocks from the house. Then, we will separate. I will walk over to the house. She will stay at the car.

I will sneak into the house through the basement—the downstairs window can be opened from the outside. I'll sneak in through that window. Once I am inside, Lana will call the landlord on the telephone from a public pay phone. He will answer if he is in the house. She will pretend to be a police circuit board operator informing him that his car has been stolen. Although this does not make sense, we both believe it will make him leave the house to look at his car. At that point, I will pour gasoline over the contents of the room in which my aunt's possessions lie. I will set fire to them and to the house, and I will escape back out the basement window. I will travel on foot to the rendezvous point where Lana will be waiting with the car. She will drive us back to her house where we will leave the car. She will leave the keys in the car and a note to her mom on the dash. We will walk down to the bus station and catch a bus out of town. I think we are both frightened about what will happen, but it feels good. The ticket will take us clear across the country. Stay in one place too long and you become a mark.

Anyway—what else is there to do. Everyone's always shouting, hurry up, hurry up. For once, we will.

GOODBYE

Lana is drunk. I am driving her car and I am not a good driver. We are going down Smith Street past the Wentworth building and I am hoping desperately that the police do not stop us because the only license I have is someone else's and I don't think it will pass muster.

We turn on to Gedding, and then on to Seventeenth. We pass up Wilson and I see a good spot. I do some shitty semblance of a parking job. The gas can is in the back. I grab it and start to head out.

Hey, Lana shouts. Come here.

What.

Listen, before a fight, the cornermen slap the boxer in the face, I think, to get them motivated.

How do you know that?

My brother used to watch boxing a lot.

Okay.

Lana slaps me in the face.

That's awful. Why would they do that?

I don't know. I'm starting the stopwatch.

Here I go.

I am standing opposite the house where I lived with my aunt. I came here when I had nothing for the first time. Now I have even less.

As I stand here, I have a change of heart. Now I just want to burn the garage. Maybe it's just nerves. But it is against the rules. No changing the plan for dumb reasons. I check to see no one is watching and cross the street. I duck into the garden. The windows of the back wall of the house are looking down at me, but they're blind.

The garden is overwhelming. I didn't figure I would be affected by it, but I feel my aunt's presence there. I am not a ghost person, but I am saying, when I see the garden I remember her clearly, unerringly. She is standing there touching the plants with her papery hands. But, I don't stop. I go to the basement window and wrench at it. It opens.

The sun is setting, and there are long shadows that run back and forth across the yard. I can see the garage, but it is dark inside. That whole part of my life is growing darker, and I know that it will never get more light. That's what the world is—we pass beyond things, and they grow dark to us, and one day we can no longer see them, not even the outlines.

I climb through the window. I pull myself down into the basement and then come back up for the gas can. I have to stand on a chair to reach it. To me it seems like I am making too much noise, so I try to be quiet for a minute, but then the sound of my own heart and my breathing is tremendous, and I start sweating.

Keep going. The basement is mostly blacked out now that the sun is low, and I stumble across it to the stairs. The floor feels wet, but I am wearing sneakers. I can't possibly feel the floor.

I make it up the stairs. Time is passing. I feel intensely sick, but not sick anywhere, not sick in my stomach, not a headache, just sick. I am shaking all over. I stand there trembling and I realize I haven't been breathing. I take a breath and as I do, I hear a phone ringing on the floor above.

The phone rings and rings. It rings and rings. It rings and it stops ringing. I freeze. I am there on the stairs, breathing and trying to hold my breath listening.

The phone starts up again. It rings and it rings. I hear footsteps. Someone answers it.

Hello.

I can't make out exactly what's said, but I hear more footsteps. I hear a noise, maybe the phone being set down. Then footsteps toward the front door. I hear locks, and the front door opens and closes.

Lana. You lovely drunk.

I rush up the stairs and open the door and am practically
blinded by the daylight that's left there. I look to the
front door, which is still closed, and cut around the corner
into the hall. There's an open door—some kind of den.
I see the wedding dress slung over an ottoman. The suit's
underneath it. I lay the dress out on the floor. Next to it
I lay out the suit. The framed photo's there, so I put it in
between. My aunt's face stares up at me. She's holding his
hand and looking at me, here, in this blighted little room.
I wonder what she thinks.

The old man's house strikes me differently now than

when I first saw it. I can see that he must have lived
here forever. But, seeing my aunt's dress piled like some
kind of prize stiffens me up. This is just a beginning.
I have nothing against this guy, even if he will call
the police on anyone, on every last person in town.
It makes me sad to think of. There are so many like him.
Each fire is a small thing. I am just beginning a long
process. I am coming into a kind of inheritance. I
can't be the only one. There must be thousands
like me.

This is it, this is it, I tell my aunt. I undo the nozzle on
the gas can and start pouring it liberally back and forth
all over the room. There is plenty of gas, and the room
stinks. My hands are shaking and I almost drop the can,
but I keep on. I step back. I am breathing through a
bandanna. I guess this is what a funeral looks like.

Come on now, come on. I peel off my right glove and take my dad's zippo out of the pocket of my hoodie. My hand is shaking even more, but I flick the zippo open. I step to the door. I take another uneasy step back out of the room.

I raise myself up as if to ask a question. I say goodbye to things like aunts, fathers.

I will leave this place. I will set out running, and maybe Lana will go with me. We will head for some corner of the earth where we can survive what we are, what we've done, what's been done to us. It will probably be a place a lot like this one. I don't know. I am not pessimistic. I just look at my future and I'm snow-blind.

Here's a prediction. This is what I think will happen, and it kills me.

I will leave here, like it's nothing. I will leave it behind, really leave it behind. I won't come back, and no one will know where I went. It will have to be that way. I will leave and I will be gone.

A week will pass, another week, a month, a year— who knows how long, and then:

My mom will still be alive. She will be sitting in her fucking chair at the Home. She'll be down by the fish pond, god knows she loves it there, and it will be a day like any other, but on this day, something will change. The sun will burn into her eyes one way or another. Some clouds will pass over with a deformed shape. An unexpected noise will reach her ears. Somehow, who knows how: she will wake up. She will shake herself. She will look around and suddenly she will know who she is. She will remember everything and she will look for me. She will say my name with her bedraggled little mouth, *Lucia, Lucia,* but I will be so far away then, I won't be able to hear her. She'll call, *Lucia, Lucia.*

She'll call to me with a voice I know, but such a thing I will never hear.

E N D

ACKNOWLEDGMENTS

My thanks to:

GGG, and some who read the manuscript when it appeared: Sasha Beilinson, Irene Beilinson, Jesse Stiles, John Francis, Jim McManus.

Jenny Jackson and all at Pantheon.

Becky Sweren and all at Kuhn Projects.

Everyone at Ch'ava in Chicago where the book was written.

A NOTE ABOUT THE AUTHOR

Jesse Ball is the author of five previous novels, including *Silence Once Begun, A Cure for Suicide,* and *Samedi the Deafness.* He is the recipient of numerous awards, including an NEA Creative Writing Fellowship for 2014 and the 2008 Paris Review Plimpton Prize. He is on the faculty at the School of the Art Institute of Chicago.

A NOTE ON THE TYPE

This book was set in Charter, the first digital typeface designed at Bitstream by Matthew Carter in 1987. Charter is a revival of eighteenth-century Roman type forms with narrow proportions and a large x-height.

Typeset by Scribe, Philadelphia, Pennsylvania
Printed and bound by Berryville Graphics, Berryville, Virginia
Designed by Maggie Hinders